Haravardhana

Nágánanda

Or The Joy of the Snakeworld a Buddist Drama in Five Acts Translated Into

English Prose, with Explanatory Notes

Haravardhana

Nágánanda
Or The Joy of the Snakeworld a Buddist Drama in Five Acts Translated Into English Prose, with Explanatory Notes

ISBN/EAN: 9783337383541

Printed in Europe, USA, Canada, Australia, Japan

Cover: Foto ©Andreas Hilbeck / pixelio.de

More available books at **www.hansebooks.com**

NÁGÁNANDA

OR

THE JOY OF THE SNAKE-WORLD.

A Buddhist Drama in Five Acts.

TRANSLATED INTO ENGLISH PROSE, WITH EXPLANATORY
NOTES, FROM THE SANSKRIT OF ŚRÍ-HARSHA-DEVA.

BY

PALMER BOYD, B.A.
SANSKRIT SCHOLAR OF TRINITY COLLEGE, CAMBRIDGE.

With an Introduction
BY
PROFESSOR COWELL.

LONDON:
TRÜBNER & CO., 60 PATERNOSTER ROW.
1872.

PREFACE.

THE Nágánanda, the sister-play to the Ratnávalí, was edited in Calcutta in 1864, by an old student of the Sanskrit College, Mádhava Chandra Ghosha. MS. copies of it are rather scarce, and Professor Wilson does not mention it in his notices of untranslated plays at the end of the "Hindu Drama." By Dr Hall's assistance, however, I procured two copies from the North-west, and these, with one or two MSS. from Bengal, enabled the editor to print an accurate text. Mr Boyd, a Cambridge pupil of mine, has now prepared an English translation; and I have been asked, by way of preface, to give some account of the date and authorship of the book.

The play is several times quoted, like the Ratnávalí, in the Sáhitya-darpana (pp. 89, 184, 189, and 249), and in the Dasa-rúpa (pp. 64, 65, 74, 178).* Dhananjaya, the

* I do not distinguish between the text of the Das'a-rúpa and the Commentary, as I feel sure that if Dhananjaya, the son of Vishnu, the author of the one, was not the same person as Dhanika, the son of Vishnu, the author of the other, they were at any rate brothers, and so the chronological value of the two remains unaltered. There is no hint given of any difference of authorship, and the two works read everywhere as if they were from the same pen, like the

b

author of the Dasa-rúpa, flourished at the court of King
Munja ; and as no other sovereign of that name occurs
in any known list of kings, this is no doubt the uncle
and predecessor of Bhoja of Dhárá. We know, from a
date given in a Jaina poem (Colebrooke, Essays, II. 53),
that Munja was reigning A.D. 993. Dhananjaya's date
is also confirmed by the fact that Hemachandra, who
lived A.D. 1174, quotes the Dasa-rúpa, in his Commentary on his own Abhidhána-chintámani, which proves
that the author was then of sufficient antiquity to be
taken as an authority in a grammarian's work. The
Ratnávalí is also quoted in the *Saraswatí-kanthábharana*,
which is ascribed to King Bhoja, who reigned in the
beginning of the eleventh century. The Ratnávalí,
therefore, and the Nágánanda, and the King S'rí Harsha
Deva, who is mentioned as their author, must be placed
in an earlier period than that of Bhoja or his uncle
Munja. This at once shows that Wilson's conjecture is
untenable, that the S'rí Harsha of the Ratnávalí could
have been the Harsha Deva of Cashmir, who reigned
from A.D. 1113 to 1125.

Dr Hall has given some good reasons for his adjudica-
tion of the Ratnávalí to the poet Bána. He was for-
tunate enough to obtain three MSS. of Bána's poem, the
Harsha-charitra (alluded to in the Sáhitya-darpana, p.
210), and in it he found the well-known verse beginning
dwípa'd anyasmád api, with which the first act of the
Ratnávalí opens. It is hardly likely that any one but

text and commentary of the Sáhitya-darpana. I may, however,
add, that Dhanika is quoted by name in the Sáhitya-darpana, p.
118 (cf. Dasa-rúpa, p. 171).

the author himself would have been guilty of the plagiarism. It is true that the author of the Kávya-prakáśa, in his enumeration of the advantages of poetry, after mentioning Kálidása as an instance of its procuring fame, brings forward, as an instance of its procuring wealth, Dhávaka in his relation with King Srí Harsha; and most of his commentators add that this poet composed the Ratnávalí under that king's name. Dr Hall, however, has shown that one commentator reads Bána instead of Dhávaka; and I need hardly add that these oral traditions, like those current about Kálidása, Vararuchi, and Chaura, are of but little historical value. The author of the Sáhitya Sára improves upon his predecessors by relating that Dhávaka was excessively poor, in spite of the learning which he had obtained by the virtue of a certain Mantra; at last, however, he composed the *Naishadhíya*, in one hundred cantos, and on showing it to King Srí Harsha, received a large jágír as his reward.* But the Naishadhíya, as will be seen in the sequel, belongs to a different Srí Harsha. The story no doubt has a certain foundation of truth, but its exact details, as in all popular legends, waver and dissolve into mist directly we touch them.

The Ratnávalí and the Nágánanda would at first sight seem to belong to the same author; half the prologue is the same in each, as also the stanza where the manager says that Srí Harsha is a clever poet, and the subject of the play attractive; but there is little similarity in the plays themselves. Of course their subjects

* The author adds as his authority—*iti vriddhair upákhydyate*, "thus it is related by the elders."

are very different, and we might expect to find even
the same author assuming different styles when treating
an heroic legend like the Nágánanda, and a genteel
comedy of domestic manners like the Ratnávalí. But
the difference in the religion of the two plays is a strong
argument against identity of authorship; and I can
hardly believe that the same poet could have written
the invocations to Buddha and to S'iva, though I hope
to be able to show that the same king may have put
them forth under his name. If I might be allowed to
venture a conjecture amidst such uncertainty, I should
claim (with Dr Hall) the Ratnávalí for Bána, the well-
known author of the Kádambarí; but I should be in-
clined to attribute the Buddhist play to the Dhávaka
mentioned in the Kávya-prakáśa. It is true that not a
solitary fragment of poetry is attributed to an author of
that name. "About a dozen unprinted collections, in
which some five hundred names of authors are adduced,
have been diligently explored in quest of Dhávaka, but
without success."* But Brahmanical memory might
easily drop a Buddhist poet, or retain only a confused
idea of his works. In this way the brief legend preserved in the Kávya-prakáśa may be right as to the poet's
name, but the commentators may be wrong in their mention of the Ratnávalí instead of the Nágánanda.

Dr Hall has thrown considerable light on the time
when Bána and the king who patronised him flourished,
by his discovery of the Harsha-charitra. In this poem
Bána celebrates the family and reign of his patron

* Dr Hall's Preface to Vásavadattá, p. 17. Cf. B.A.S. Journ. 1862.

Harsha or Harsha-vardhana, and the history agrees so remarkably with that given in Hiouen Thsang of Harsha-vardhana, or Síladitya,[*] the King of Kanouj, in the first half of the seventh century, that we can hardly feel any doubt as to their being the same person.

Now Hiouen Thsang's account of the court of Kanouj may throw some light on these dramas. Whether they were really written by the same poet or not, they profess to be the composition of the same king; and the similarity of much of the prologue, and the identity of one of the verses, give an external appearance of identity of authorship in spite of the difference in the style; and this may have been part of the deception practised on the audience. Bána may have afterwards inserted a verse from the Ratnávalí in his unfinished Harsha-charitra, as a tacit assertion of his claim to the authorship of that work, just as Sostratus is said to have engraved his own name beneath the royal inscription on the Pharos. Still the difficulty remains as to the Hindu and Buddhist character of the plays; and I think this is much better explained by the character of the king than by assuming such an almost unparalleled versatility of faith in a poet.

Hiouen Thsang is loud in his praises of Harsha-vardhana's devotion to Buddhism; but surely his own narrative is sufficient to warn us against taking these eulogies too literally. The king may have built the hundreds of stúpas along the Ganges, he may have

---

erected the almshouses for the poor, and the resting-
places for pilgrims; and there can be no doubt that he
favoured the Buddhist faith, and presided at their as-
semblies, and honoured their holy men. But in the
descriptions of the two great convocations, at which
Hiouen Thsang was present, we can see that the king
was by no means the thorough Buddhist which we
might have expected. In the first, twenty tributary
princes take a part, and each brings with him the most
distinguished Buddhist and Brahman doctors in his
realm, and both parties are welcomed with the same
hospitality; and though we only read of the homage
paid to a golden statue of Buddha, we can hardly
believe that, with all these Brahman guests invited,
there was no other ceremony. But in the second convocation, which is described in Hiouen Thsang's life by
his disciples, we have a fuller account. This was held
at Prayága, at the confluence of the Jumna and Ganges;
eighteen kings were present, and five hundred thousand
monks and laymen. The first day they installed the
statue of Buddha, the second day the statue of the Sun,
and the third day that of Maheśwara, so that the king's
official patronage was shared by the Brahmans even
more than by the Buddhists. Similarly at the distributions of alms, we read that on the fourth day the king
distributed his bounty to twenty thousand Buddhist
ascetics; but we read immediately afterwards, that similar distributions were made to the Brahmans and other
heretics, and these lasted respectively twenty and ten
days; and last of all, the nirgranthas, or naked mendi-
cants (who were especially disliked by the Buddhists, cf.

Burnouf, *Introd.*, p. 312), came in for their share, for ten days. Now this narrative seems to reveal a state of things which would completely account for these two plays. Hiouen Thsang expressly says of the kingdom of Kanouj, that half the inhabitants held "the true doctrine," and half were attached to "error;" and no doubt a similar division existed to a greater or less extent in each of the subject kingdoms. We have only to suppose some such convocation at Kanouj as these which he has described; and what more natural than that the tributary princes, whom the manager mentions in the prologue, should, on the day of the Buddhist ceremonies, witness the Nágánanda, with its invocatory stanzas to Jina, and, on the day of installing the image of Maheśwara, should witness the Ratnávalí, with its opening Nándís to S'iva? The Málatí-mádhava of Bhavabhúti (who flourished at Kanouj about A.D. 720) presents the same toleration of the two rival religions; the play is Hindu, and the Nándí is addressed to S'iva, but a female Buddhist ascetic, with one of her disciples, is a leading character; she is the nurse of the heroine, and the confidante of her father the minister, in his desire to marry his daughter to the son of an old friend, and Mádhava, the young hero, studies logic in Buddhist schools.*

* We know that the Buddhists paid great attention to the study of logic, from the frequent references in Hiouen Thsang to *hetu-vidyá*, "the science of reasons." In a passage which I have quoted from the *Nyáya-várttika-tátparya-tíká*, in the preface to my translation of the Kusumánjali, Váchaspati-mis'ra states that the Nyáya-s'ástra was originally delivered by Akshapáda, or Gotama, and completed by Pakshila-swámin, and that Uddyotakara compiled his Várttika, or "Annotations," in order to clear away the

There can be no doubt, I think, that the King Srí
Harsha Deva of our two plays is a different person from
the Srí Harsha who wrote the Naishadha and the
Kha*nd*ana-Kha*nda*-Khádya, as the latter, in the closing
verses of both works, speaks of himself as the dependant
of the king of Kanouj, and boasts of the allowance
of betel granted him at the court. His age is un-,
certain. Bábú Rájendra lál Mitra (B.A.S. Journ. 1864)
has conjectured that he may have been the Srí Harsha,
who, according to tradition, was one of the five Kanouj
Brahmans who were invited into Bengal by Ádi Súr, in
the tenth century. His chief arguments are that the
author of the Naishadha names among his works a
"description of the sea," and "a history of the kings
of Bengal." But I find, from a notice in the first num-
ber of the "Indian Antiquary," that Dr Bühler of Bom-
bay has recently fixed his date in the twelfth century.

The story of the Nágánanda is no doubt a Buddhist
legend. It is found twice in the Kathá-sarit-ságara, in
which are incorporated so many legends of Buddhist
origin. In chapter xxii., we have a version which gives
the latter part of the story as it is told in the two last
acts, but the earlier acts are only alluded to; but in
chapter xc., in the Vetála book, we have a second
version, which follows the whole play very closely.
Thus Malayavatí's singing at the temple is described
as in the first act; the love-scenes of the second are

erroneous interpretations of *Ding-nága* and others. Ding-nága was
a celebrated Buddhist teacher, and his logical works are still ex-
tant, see Prof. Weber's Note, Zeitschrift d. Morgenl. Gesellschaft,
xxii. 727.

also imitated, and we have the same sentiment as in the fourth, where Jímútaváhana wonders that the King of Snakes, with all his thousand mouths, had not even one wherewith to offer himself as a victim to save his subjects. In śl. 197, we have evidently an allusion to the name of the play,—the bones of the dead snakes are brought to life again, and it is said,

" Te 'pi sarve samuttasthus tad-varánṛrita-jívitáḥ ;
Surair Nágair muni-gaṇaiḥ sánandair militair atha
Sa loka-tritayábhikhyám babhára Malayáchalaḥ."

Mr Boyd has pointed out in his notes the allusions in the play to Buddhist doctrines. Professor Wilson remarks, in the Introduction to his translation of the Mrichchhakaṭiká, "Many centuries have elapsed since Hindu writers were acquainted with the Buddhists in their genuine characters ; their tenets are preserved in philosophical treatises with something like accuracy, but any attempt to describe their persons and practices invariably confounds them with the Jainas ;" and this very confusion occurs in the Mudrá-rákshasa, which he attributes to the twelfth century. But the present drama is correct in its allusions, which may be another argument in favour of the comparatively early date which I have advocated.

The two last acts are in the true style of Buddhist invention ; but I do not remember to have seen any direct reference to Jímútaváhana in any Buddhist legend. Burnouf mentions (*Introd.*, p. 620) that, though the *gośírsha* sandal is frequently alluded to in Buddhist books, he had only found one allusion to the

chandana of Malaya. This occurred in a legend of the
Suvarna-prabhása, which relates how a prince gave his
body to feed a hungry tigress. But there is a distinct
reference to some such legend as that of our drama, in
the second Nepalese Buddhist tract translated by Wilson,
in the 16th vol. of the " Asiatic Researches." We read
there, " May the holy Tírtha be propitious to you, where
the Nága obtained rest from Társkshya (Garuda)." This
is explained by the Nepalese as referring to a local shrine
called Gokarna, but it no doubt originally referred to the
far more celebrated Gokarna of Malabar. The Nágas play
an important part in many Buddhist legends (as, for instance, in that of Sangha-rakshita); and Mr Fergusson
has shown that they are introduced in the Buddhist
sculptures at Sanchi and Amaravati, and in the latter
as objects of worship. The description of the Nágas
in the fifth act, with their human forms, but scaly skins
and three hoods, singularly agrees with some of the
drawings in his book.

The appearance of the goddess Gaurí is a curious
feature of the drama, and seems to point to that gradual
mixture of Buddhist with S'aiva notions, which we find
fully developed int he Tantras of Nepal. There female
S'aiva deities, such as Durgá, Mahákálí, &c., are continually invoked to grant protection to the Buddhist wor-
shipper. Wilson supposes that the Tantras were introduced into Nepal between the seventh and twelfth
centuries, but Burnouf has pointed out some traces of
S'aiva influence even in the " Lotus de la bonne Loi,"
and other " developed Sútras."   E. B. COWELL.

" Wohlwollen und Erbarmen, oder genauer allgemeine Wesensliebe ist der positive Kern der buddhistischen Moral."

Koeppen.

DRAMATIS PERSONÆ.

<hr>

MEN.

Jímútavhana, the hero, a prince of the Vidyádharas or celestial choristers.

Jímútaketu, his father, king of the Vidyádharas.

Vis'vávasu, king of the Siddhas.

Mitrávasu, his son.

Sankhachúda, a prince of the Nágas or snake deities.

Garuda, king of the birds and mortal foe of the Nágas.

Átreya, a Brahman, the vidúshaka or king's jester.

The *Vita*, or parasite.

Sunanda, the doorkeeper.

The Chamberlain.

A Slave.

A *Nága* attendant.

WOMEN.

The Goddess *Gaurí*.

The Queen of the Vidyádharas, mother of *Jímútaváhana*.

Malayavatí, daughter of Vis'vávasu.

Chaturíká, her attendant.

Sankhachúda's mother.

Several female attendants.

<hr>

The scene lies partly in the Palace of the Siddha King, and partly on the Mountains of Malabar.

THE NÁGÁNANDA.

Prologue.

NÁNDÍ, OR OPENING BENEDICTION.*

" Of whom dost thou think, putting on a pretence of
religious abstraction, yet opening for an instant thine
eyes? See! saviour though thou art, thou dost not protect us, sick with the shafts of Love. Falsely art thou
compassionate. Who is more cruel than thou?"

May Buddha, the conqueror, who was thus jealously
addressed by the nymphs of Mára,† protect you!

---

* Every Sanskrit play opens with one or more Nándís, or bene-
dictions, in which the blessing of some deity is invoked upon the
audience. This is the only instance in Sanskrit literature where the
power thus invoked is Buddha.

† One of the most celebrated scenes in the mythic history of
Buddha is his temptation under the Bodhi tree by Mára, the
Buddhist Eros, corresponding to the Hindu Káma. Mára at first
attempted to frighten him by legions of armed warriors; failing in
this, he tried to seduce him by his daughters, the Apsarasas. The
sage, however, endures both temptations with unruffled equanimity,
and eventually the tempter retires utterly baffled.—*See Lalita-
Vistara,* ch. xxi.

A

Again,

May the Lord of Munis protect you! who, lost in reflection, and filled with transcendent knowledge, was seen to be utterly unmoved by Indra,[*] whose every hair was on end through astonishment; by the Siddhas,[†] their heads bent low in obeisance; by the nymphs, whose eyes quivered, as they alternately smiled, yawned, trembled, and frowned; by the heroes of Mára, dancing with harshly-beaten drums; and by Mára himself, who had drawn his bow to the full!

(At the conclusion of the benediction)—

STAGE MANAGER.

Enough of this prolixity. To-day, at the feast of Indra, I was thus addressed by the company of kings, who have arrived from various countries, dependants on the lotus feet of the noble King S'rí-harsha-deva, after they had summoned me respectfully, "That play named Nágánanda, connected with the sovereign of the celestial choristers,[‡] and adorned with a new arrangement of the incidents by our Lord, S'rí-harsha-deva, has been heard of by us through successive report, but has never been seen by us on the stage; therefore you should perform it to-day with suitable dramatic appliances, both

---

[*] In the Buddhist mythology, Indra is the king of the lowest heaven but one; Mára being located in the sixth or highest, and having more or less influence over all the beings beneath him.

[†] Siddha, a divine person of undefined attributes and character—a sort of demigod or spirit, inhabiting, together with the Vidyá-dharas, Munis, &c., the region between the earth and the sun.—*See Wilson's Dictionary.*

[‡] *i.e.* Vidyádharas.

through your respect for that great king, who rejoices the hearts of all people, and through your willingness to oblige us." Therefore, after I have adjusted my attire, I will carry out this request. (*Walking and looking about.*) I have no doubt that I have won the hearts of all the spectators, since S'rí-harsha-deva is a clever poet ; and this assembly are good judges of merit. The history of the king of the Siddhas is very attractive in the world, and we ourselves are skilful actors. Each of these things by itself would be sufficient for success ; how much more the whole assemblage of them, brought together by my accumulation of good luck ! So, after I have gone to my house and called my wife, I will commence the entertainment. (*Walking about, looking towards the tiring room.*) Here is my house. I will enter. (*After entering.*) O lady, come here a moment !

An ACTRESS (*entering in tears*).

My lord, here am I, unlucky one that I am, let the son of my lord say what is to be done.

MANAGER (*looking at* ACTRESS).

O lady, why do you thus weep unreasonably, when the Nágánanda is to be performed ?

ACTRESS.

Sir, how should I not weep, since just now my father, having discovered that he is old, and influenced by a sudden disgust for the world, saying to himself, "Art *thou* fit to support the duties of a household ?" is gone with his wife to a sacred grove ?

MANAGER (*in distraction*).

What! How! My two parents, leaving me, are gone to a sacred grove? What is now seemly to be done? (*After thinking.*) But how shall I remain at home, giving up the pleasure of attendance on my father? For, in order to perform the service of my father, I will quit the possessions fallen to my lot, and go off this day to the forest, as did Jímútaváhana.*

[*Exeunt.*

END OF PROLOGUE.

ACT I.

Then enter JÍMÚTAVÁHANA *and the* VIDÚSHAKA.

JÍMÚTAVÁHANA
(*in a tone of apathy towards the world*).

O friend, Átreya, well do I know that youth is an abode of passion. I am certain that it is transient. Who in the world does not know that it is averse to investigation of right and wrong? Yet, worthless as it is, it may still be used for the attainment of the desired end, if it is thus spent by me, devotedly obeying my parents.

VIDÚSHAKA (*with vexation*).

Alas, my friend, no wonder you are despondent, en-

---

* The Hindu dramatists always endeavour to connect the business of the prologue with that of the main action. The spectator thus gradually passes from the real world in which the actors live, to the imaginary one in which the personages of the drama move.

during the annoyance of living for so long a time in the forest, for the sake of these two, who are already half dead. So now do me a favour. Having turned aside from the strictness of your attendance on your father, let the pleasure of sovereignty, sweet through the attainment of every wish, be tasted by you.

JÍMÚTAVÁHANA.

O friend, you speak not well. For, in this world, what is the splendour of one sitting on a throne compared with that of one in attendance on his father? What enjoyment is there to a king such as that of one shampooing his father's feet? What satisfaction in enjoying the whole world, such as in eating a father's leavings? Sovereignty is in fact only a trouble to one who has deserted his father. Is there one good thing in it?

VIDÚSHAKA (aside).

Bother his "penchant" for waiting on his father! (After considering.) Never mind. I will put it to him in this way. (Aloud.) O friend, I do not in truth speak only of the enjoyment of sovereignty. There is another thing which you should do.

JÍMÚTAVÁHANA (smiling).

O friend, has not all that should have been done, been done? See here. My subjects are placed in the right path; the virtuous are happy; my relatives are placed on an equality with myself, and a regency is made in the kingdom; to the poor man a tree of Paradise has been . given, whose fruit gives even more than he wishes for.

Say, what more than this should be done? or what remains in your mind?

VIDÚSHAKA.

O friend, your enemy, the base Matanga, is very daring; and, whilst he is at hand, the kingdom, though duly governed by the prime minister, does not, in your absence, appear very firmly settled.

JÍMÚTAVÁHANA.

Fie! O fool, dost thou fear that Matanga will seize the kingdom?

VIDÚSHAKA.

What else?

JÍMÚTAVÁHANA.

If even it were so, why should it not be? Is not all I possess, even to my very body, kept for the benefit of others? That it is not given up to him of my own accord is through compliance with my father. What, then, is the use of this pointless consideration? Better that the command of my father be at once undertaken. "O my child Jímútaváhana," he said, "by the spending of many days here this place has its flowers, kuśa-grass, and fuel used up, and its rice, plants, fruits, and roots well-nigh consumed, therefore go hence to the Malaya* mountain, and seek there for a hermitage suited for our occupation." Come, then, let us go to the Malaya mountain.

* Malaya — the Western Ghâts — whence the name Malabar (malaya-vara).

VIDÚSHAKA.

Whatever your highness orders. Let your highness come.

[*Both walk about.*

VIDÚSHAKA (*looking in advance*).

O friend! see, see! Here in good truth comes the wind from Malaya, which removes the fatigue of the journey, like the clasping of the neck of the long-desired loved one on first meeting,—bearing cool showers of drops, caught up from the cascade as it falls broken from the crystal rocks, and strongly fragrant through its contact with the mountain slopes, covered with groves of dense and juicy sandal trees; it thrills every limb of your body.

JÍMÚTAVÁHANA (*looking with surprise*).

Ah! we have already reached the Malaya hill. (*Looking all round.*) Oh, how pleasant it is! Inasmuch as this Malaya hill, with its sandal exuding from the wounds made by the mighty elephants as they rub their cheeks in their passion against the trunks, and with the fastnesses of its caves resounding when lashed by the ocean waves, and with its rocks of pearl stained by the foot-dye of the women of the Siddhas as they pass—the sight of it gives to my mind some longing for the joys of earth. Come, we will ascend and seek for some suitable site for a hermitage.

VIDÚSHAKA.

Let us do so. (*Standing in advance.*) Let your highness come on.

[*They ascend.*

JÍMÚTAVÁHANA (*starting from a throbbing of his right eye*).[*]

My right eye throbs, though I have no object of desire. Yet the saying of the wise cannot prove false. What, then, can this portend?

VIDÚSHAKA.

It shows undoubtedly that some loved object is at hand.

JÍMÚTAVÁHANA.

It must be as you say.

VIDÚSHAKA (*looking on all sides*).

O friend, look! look! Here in good truth is all the appearance of an ascetic grove, resplendent with unusually thick and dense trees, its crowd of young animals reclining at ease unalarmed, and its smoke freely issuing laden with scent from the sacrificial ghee.

JÍMÚTAVÁHANA.

You conjecture rightly. This *is* an ascetic grove. The bark of the trees is stripped off for clothing, though not in too wide strips, as if out of pity for them. The pure water of the cascade has broken fragments of old waterpots[†] just visible at the bottom; and here and there appear the broken girdles of munja grass[‡] cast off

---

[*] The Hindus believe that the throbbing of the right eye or arm is a good omen for a man, but of the left, a bad omen. The reverse of this holds in the case of a woman.

[†] Compare Manu II. 64:—."His girdle, his deerskin, his staff, his sacrificial cord, and his waterpot, he must throw into the water when they are worn out, and take others with sacred texts."

[‡] Munja-grass, the *Saccharum munja*, from the fibres of which the string is prepared to form the thread worn by the Brahmans. Manu II. 43.

by the young Brahmans; whilst a verse of the Sáma Veda is recited by a parrot, who has learnt it from constantly hearing it. Come, then, we will enter and look about us.

[*They enter.*

JÍMÚTAVÁHANA (*looking about, with astonishment*).

Oh, the tranquil charms of an ascetic grove! The basins at the foot of the young trees are kept full by the daughters of the hermits. Its fuel is cut fresh and fresh .by the reciting pupils, whilst the detail of the doubtful passages of the Veda is constantly discussed by the Munis, who delight in the task. Even these trees, taught respect for a guest, seem to utter a sweet welcome with the murmuring of bees, and make, so to speak, an obeisance with their heads bowed down with fruit; sprinkling a rain of flowers, they present me, as it were, a propitiatory offering. Hence this ascetic grove is well suited for a dwelling place. I think we shall have peace while living here.

VIDÚSHAKA.

What is this, friend? The deer, with their necks a little bent, the mouthfuls of darbha grass falling half-chewed from their motionless mouths, their eyes tranquilly closed in complete content, seem to listen with one ear pricked up.

JÍMÚTAVÁHANA (*after listening*).

Friend, you have seen correctly; for these antelopes, their bodies bent sideways, stopping the noise of chewing the mouthfuls of darbha grass between their teeth, listen to the distinct melodious words of a song, possessing, through due regard to the laws of harmony, the treble and bass tones impartially developed from their respective organs,* mingled with the notes of the strings of the resounding lute, as with the hum of bees.

VIDÚSHAKA.

Who, then, my friend, sings here in the sacred grove?

JÍMÚTAVÁHANA.

Inasmuch as these notes sound clearly, struck by the tips of soft fingers, I conjecture that it is sung with Kákilí† for its key-note. (*Pointing forwards with his*

---

* This passage is difficult, as it alludes to some technicalities of Hindu music. The Hindus place the bass (mandra), the tenor (madhya), and the treble (tára), in the chest, throat, and top of the palate respectively. Thus the Sangíta-ratnákara, "iti vastu-sthitis távad gáue tredhá bhaved asau ; *hridi*, mandro ; gale, mad-hyo ; múrdhni, tara ; iti kramát." Compare Prof. Aufrecht's Catalogue of Oxford MSS., 200 *b* 3.

† Kákilí is explained as a sweet soft sound, corresponding to the cuckoo's note. Hindu poets give to the kokila, or cuckoo, the fifth note of their scale. Compare Browning:—

> " Here 's the spring back, or close,
>   When the almond blossom blows,
>   We shall have the word
>   In that minor third
>   There is none but the cuckoo knows ;
>   Heaps of the guelder-rose,—
> I must bear with it, I suppose."

Which is curiously paralleled by a verse quoted in the Sáhitya Darpana :—

"The bees may fill every quarter with the sound of their hum-

finger.) In this temple some goddess plays the lute in propitiation of a deity.

VIDÚSHAKA.

Come, friend, let us too see the temple of the god.

JÍMÚTAVÁHANA.

You say well. The gods should be revered. (*Going up quickly, stopping.*) But perhaps we are not worthy to look. Let us then enter this tamála shrub, and wait for an opportunity.

[*They do so.*

Then enter seated on the ground,* playing a lute, MALAY-AVATÍ, *and a* SERVANT GIRL.

MALAYAVATÍ (*sings*).

O adored Gaurí, resplendent as with white pollen from the filaments of full-blown lotuses, may my desire be accomplished by thy favour!

JÍMÚTAVÁHANA (*after hearing it*).

O friend, a capital song! and first-rate music! Distinctness is attained, even though she plays with her bare fingers; † good time is kept, clearly defined in due

---

mings; and the breeze, rising from the groves of sandalwood, may gently approach; the playful tame cuckoos on the mango's top may make their musical fifth note; but may my vital spirit, hard as adamant, quickly go from me—let it be gone." Comm. on (215).

* This was managed by drawing aside a curtain or drop-scene.

† Literally, "Distinctness is attained by the organ of touch, though it be tenfold," meaning that the playing was clear, though she played without the metal instrument which they generally use.

divisions of slow, medium, and quick; the three pauses
are rendered in proper order with the "gopuchchha"
first; the three modes of playing are fully shown in the
slow and quick accompaniments.*

GIRL (*affectionately*).

O princess, you have been playing for a long time.
How is it that your fingers are not tired?

MALAYAVATÍ (*reproachfully*).

Girl, how should my fingers be weary, when playing
before the goddess?

GIRL.

O princess, in my opinion there is little use in playing
before this cruel one, who, up to this time, shows no
favour to you; though you have been so long a time
conciliating her with due observances, which come hard
on a young girl.

VIDÚSHAKA.

It is only a girl after all.   Why should we not look?

JÍMÚTAVÁHANA.

What harm would there be in so doing? Women
may be looked at without sin.   Yet, perhaps, if she

---

* Here again there is difficulty from the continual reference to
musical technicalities, and the translation is only conjectural.
The yati-trayam occurs in the Márkaṇḍeya Puráṇa, xxiii. 54.   I
have corrected the reading in the fourth line from *tattwodyánugatás*
to *tattwaughánugatás*, from Daśa-rúpa, p. 178, where the passage is
quoted; tattwa is "slow," ogha "quick" time.

saw us, through fear, which is easily excited in one at her time of life, and of her character, she would not remain long here. So we will simply look through this network of Tamála branches.

VIDÚSHAKA.

We will do so.

[*Both of them peep through.*

VIDÚSHAKA (*after looking, with astonishment*).

O friend, see, see ! how wonderful ! Not only by her knowledge of the lute does she cause delight, but her beauty, corresponding to her skill, charms the eye. Who can she be ? Is she a goddess or a woman of the Nágas ? A princess of the Vidyádharas, or born of the family of Siddhas ?

JÍMÚTAVÁHAXA (*looking longingly*).

Friend, who it is, I know not ; but this I do know, if she be a goddess, the thousand eyes of Hari have all they can wish. If she be a woman of the Nágas, then, whilst her face is there, the lowest hell is not without its moon. If she be of the Vidyádharas, then our race surpasses all others. If she be born of a family of Siddhas, then in the three worlds are the Siddhas glorious.

VIDÚSHAKA
(*after looking at the hero, joyfully, aside*).

Good luck ! Though after a long delay, he is at last fallen into the power of love, or rather—(*looking at* *himself, and gesticulating eating)*—not so; but into the power of me single-handed, the Brahman.*

GIRL (*affectionately*).

O princess, do I not say, " Where is the use of playing before this cruel one?"

[*She throws down the lute.*

MALAYAVATÍ (*angrily*).

Girl! offend not the revered Gaurí.   Has not a favour been done me by her this very day?

GIRL (*with joy*).

O princess, what can it be?

MALAYAVATÍ.

Girl, I know it well.   To-day in a dream, as I was playing this very lute, I was thus addressed by the revered Gaurí,—" Child Malayavatí, I am well pleased with your perfect knowledge of the lute, and with your excessive devotion towards me, which is hard for a young girl; therefore before long a sovereign of the Vidyádharas shall be your husband."

GIRL (*with delight*).

If it is so, why do you call it a dream?   Has not the goddess given you the very desire of your heart?

---

* The buffoon, who, as usual, is a Brahman, seems to anticipate the pleasures of the coming wedding-feast. He feels that his master is stepping from his sublime ascetic elevation down to his own more mundane level.

VIDÚSHAKA (*having heard*).

Friend, surely this is a good opportunity to show ourselves to the princess. Come, then, we will go up.

JÍMÚTAVÁHANA.

I will not yet enter.

VIDÚSHAKA

(*going up and forcibly dragging the hero, who resists*).

Welcome to your highness! Chaturiká speaks the truth. Here is the husband promised by the goddess.

MALAYAVATÍ

(*standing up bashfully, pointing to the hero*).

Girl, who is this?

GIRL (*after looking at the hero, aside*).

From this form of his, which surpasses all others, I conjecture that he is the man given through the favour of the goddess.

[*The heroine looks at the hero wistfully, and with modesty.*

JÍMÚTAVÁHANA.

This form of thine, oh tremulous-eyed one, whose full breasts are agitated by thy breathing, is sufficiently fatigued by devotions. Why then, oh timid one, is it further distressed at my presence?

MALAYAVATÍ (*aside.*)

Through excessive alarm I cannot stand facing him.

[*Looking at the hero sideways, and with a blush, she stands somewhat turned away.*

GIRL.

Princess, what does all this mean?

MALAYAVATÍ.

I cannot remain in his neighbourhood, so come away. We will go elsewhere.

[*She wishes to rise.*

VIDÚSHAKA.

Alas! she is scared. Shall I keep her just for a moment, as I do any learning that I may have read?

JÍMÚTAVÁHANA.

Where would be the harm of it?

VIDÚSHAKA.

O lady! why this behaviour of yours in such a grove as this, that a guest just arrived is not favoured by you with a single word?

GIRL (*after looking at the heroine, to herself*).

Her eye seems pleased. I will speak to her. (*Aloud.*) O princess, the Brahman speaks fittingly. Good behaviour towards guests is becoming in you. Why, then, do you stand as if distraught in your behaviour towards so distinguished a one; or rather, remain so if you will,—I will do what is seemly. (*Addressing the hero.*) Welcome to your highness! by occupying this seat, let your highness add beauty to the spot.

VIDÚSHAKA.

Friend, she says well. Let us sit down here and rest for a moment.

JÍMÚTAVÁHANA.

You are right.

[*Both sit down.*

MALAYAVATÍ (*addressing the servant girl*).

O laughter-loving one, act not thus. Perhaps some Ascetic is looking, and he will set me down as a giddy one.

Then enters an ASCETIC.

ASCETIC.

I am thus bidden by Kauśika, the head of the family : " My child, S'ándilya, the young king of the Siddhas, Mitrávasu, is gone to-day, at his father's request, to seek Prince Jímútaváhana, the future monarch of the Vidyádharas, who is somewhere here on the Malaya Mount, as a husband for his sister Malayavatí, and perhaps the limit of the time for the mid-day oblation will pass by while Malayavatí awaits his return. Go, therefore, and fetch her with you." I am going, therefore, to the temple of Gaurí in the sacred grove.

(*Walking about, looking down on the ground, with surprise.*)

Ah ! Whose footsteps have we here on the dusty ground, having the sign of the chakra manifest? (*Looking forward and seeing Jímútavdhana.*) Assuredly it will be the footstep of this mighty man. For there is the turban-like mass of hair visible on the scalp; there shines a woolly tuft between the eyebrows;* his eyes resemble a lotus; his chest vies with Hari; and since

---

* Compare the signs of Buddha in Lalita-Vistara, ch. vii.

his feet are marked with the chakra, I conjecture that
he who rests here is assuredly one who has attained the
dignity of an emperor of the Vidyádharas.   However,
away with doubt.   It must surely be Jímútaváhana himself.   (*Seeing Malayavati.*)   Ah! here is the princess
too.   (*Looking at them both.*)   Destiny would at length
be acting in a straightforward manner did she unite this
pair, mutually suited to one another.   (*Going up and
addressing the hero.*)   Welcome to your highness!

JÍMÚTAVÁHANA.

Jímútaváhana salutes your honour.

> [*Wishes to rise.*

ASCETIC.

Do not rise; your highness should be respected by us,
for "A guest is every one's master."*   Remain, then,
at your ease.

MALAYAVATÍ.

Sir, I bow to you.

ASCETIC (*turning to her*).

My child, mayst thou marry a suitable husband!
O princess, Kauśika, the head of the family, sends word
to thee, "The time of the mid-day oblation passes by,
come therefore quickly."

MALAYAVATÍ.

As the "Guru"† orders.   (*To herself.*)   On the one
side the orders of the "Guru," on the other the pleasure

---

* Compare Hitopadésa, i. 62.   † The spiritual parent.

of the sight of the dear one. Thus my heart swings me to and fro, perched on a see-saw of going and not going.

[*Rising with a sigh, and looking at the hero with modesty and affection, she goes out with the* ASCETIC.

JÍMÚTAVÁHANA

(*with a sigh, looking longingly after the heroine*).

By her whose departure is slow, by reason of the rounded beauty of her form, an impress is stamped upon my heart, even though she leaves me.

VIDÚSHAKA.

Well, you have seen all there was to be seen! The fire of my appetite rages, its fury doubled, so to speak, by the heat of the rays of the mid-day sun. Come, then, let us go forth, that I, the Brahman, having become some one's guest, may support my life with bulbs, roots, and fruit, obtained from the Munis.

JÍMÚTAVÁHANA (*looking upwards*).

The adorable thousand-rayed one has reached the zenith ; for see, the lord of elephants with pallid checks, their sandal-juice instantaneously dried off by the excessive heat, as he fans his face with the breezes of his broad ears, his chest all wet with the drops falling from his trunk, endures a state of existence hard to be borne even by the fainting Bignonia.

[*Exeunt omnes.*

END OF THE FIRST ACT OF THE NÁGÁNANDA.

ACT II.

Then enters a SERVANT GIRL.

GIRL.

I am bidden by the Princess Malayavatí, " Mano-harikà, my respected brother, Mitrávasu, tarries long to-day; go, then, and inquire whether he has come or not." (*She walks about.*) Who can this be coming hither in such haste. (*Looking.*) Why! it is Chaturikà.

Then enters a SECOND SERVANT GIRL.

FIRST GIRL (*going up to her*).

Holla, Chaturikà! why, avoiding me, do you go thus hastily?

SECOND GIRL.

O Manoharikà, I am bidden by the Princess Malaya-vatí, " Chaturikà, my body cannot endure the fatigue of gathering flowers. My passion exceedingly torments me, as though produced by autumnal sunshine. Go, then, prepare the seat of moonstone in the arbour of sandal-creepers, shadowed with the leaves of young plantain trees." I have done as ordered, and am going to inform the princess.

FIRST GIRL.

Go, then, quickly and tell her, so that having gone thither her fever may be alleviated.

SECOND GIRL (*laughingly to herself*).

Her fever is not of a nature to be thus relieved. In

my opinion, her fever will be augmented on seeing the bower of sandal-creepers with its various delights. (*Aloud.*) Go on, then, you. I too will go and inform the princess that the moonstone seat is prepared.

[*Exeunt.*

END OF INTERLUDE.

Then enters with a longing look MALAYAVATÍ *and a* SERVANT GIRL.

MALAYAVATÍ (*with a sigh, to herself*).

O heart! after having made my mouth dumb through shyness towards him, thou art now gone to him of thine own accord. Alas! for thy selfishness! (*Aloud.*) O Chaturiká! point out to me the temple of Gaurí.

GIRL (*to herself*).

Though on the way to the bower of sandal-creepers, she says, "To the temple of Gaurí!" (*Aloud.*) The princess is on the way to the bower of young sandal-trees.

MALAYAVATÍ (*with confusion*).

It is well that you remind me. Come then, we will go thither.

GIRL.

Let the princess come.

[MALAYAVATÍ *goes to a different part of the stage.*

GIRL (*looking back with uneasiness, to herself*).

Alas, for her absence of mind! Why, she is actually gone towards the temple of the goddess! (*Aloud.*) O lady! is not the sandal-creeper bower in this direction? Come this way, then. (*The heroine does so with a meaningless smile.*)* Here we are at the sandal-creeper bower, therefore let your ladyship enter and sit down on the moonstone seat to recover yourself.

[*Both sit down.*

MALAYAVATÍ (*with a sigh, to herself*).

Lord of the flower-tipped arrows,† against that man who surpasses you in beauty of form you do nothing at all; but against me, though blameless, you are not ashamed to strike, saying to yourself, "She is a weak woman." (*Looking at herself, and gesticulating as one in love. Aloud.*) Girl, how is it that even this sandal-creeper bower, from which the sun's rays are kept by the density of the shoots, does not alleviate the pain of my fever?

GIRL.

I know the cause of this fever, but the princess is unwilling to avow it.

MALAYAVATÍ (*to herself*).

I am seen through by her. Still I will ask. (*Aloud.*) Girl, what is that which I will not avow? Come, tell me this cause of yours.

GIRL.

It is the man placed in your heart.

---

* This is one of the symptoms of love in a Hindu heroine. See Sáhitya-Darpana, sec. 151.

† Káma, the Hindu Cupid, bears a bow with its string made of bees, and its five arrows each tipped with a peculiar flower.

MALAYAVATÍ (*with joy and agitation, after rising and advancing two or three steps*).

Where—where is he?

GIRL (*rising, with a smile*).

O lady, what *he ?*

[*Heroine sitting down ashamed, keeps her face bent down.*

GIRL.

Well, I will explain. This man who is established in your affections was promised to you by the goddess in a dream, and a moment after he was seen by you, resembling Cupid without his flowery arrows. This man, then, is the cause of your anguish, so that even this bower of young sandal-trees, though cool in its very nature, does not relieve the pain of your fever.

MALAYAVATÍ (*to herself*).

I am found out by Chaturiká. (*Aloud.*) Girl, well are you named Chaturiká.* Why should I longer conceal it from you? I will tell you all.

GIRL.

O lady! it is as good as told already. Where is the use of more talk? You have had enough agitation. Do not further excite yourself. As sure as my name is Chaturiká, he too will not enjoy a moment of happiness until he has again seen you. I have found out this too.

* Chaturiká, from *chatura*, clever, expert.

MALAYAVATÍ (*with tears*).

Whence should I obtain so great bliss?

GIRL.

Say not so.   How can he be happy when even Vishnu has no happiness without Lakshmí on his bosom.

MALAYAVATÍ.

Can a friend say anything but what is kind?   But it makes my passion distress me more, when I think how I did not honour the noble hero with a single word, so that he will say to himself, "That awkward girl is wanting in respectful behaviour." (*She weeps.*)

GIRL.

O lady, do not give way!   (*To herself.*) Yet how should she not weep, since the great passion of her heart distresses her more and more?   What then shall I now do?   I will place on her breast the juice of a sandal-creeper spray.   (*Rising and plucking a sprig of sandal, and squeezing out the juice, she places it on her breast.   Aloud.*) O lady, do I not say, "Weep not?"   Even this sandal-juice, notwithstanding its nature, does not relieve thy breast, since it is rendered warm by these tear-drops falling unchecked.

[*Takes a plantain leaf and fans her.*

MALAYAVATÍ (*checks her with a hand*).

Do not fan me.   Even the wind of the plantain leaf is warm.

GIRL.

Do not impute the fault to it. It is you who make warm this wind of the plantain leaf, which is cool through its contact with the gathered sandal shoots, changing its nature with your sighs.

MALAYAVATÍ (*with tears*).

Is there any means of checking this fever?

GIRL.

There is indeed. If *he* would but now come.

Then enters the hero with the VIDÚSHAKA.

JÍMÚTAVÁHANA.

O Cupid, why are these purposeless arrows flung against me, already so deeply wounded? Since I was looked on by her, regardless of the Muni's presence, when, as she turned, though but for a moment, she caused, by the glance of her bright black eye, the trees of the hermitage to appear flecked,* as though they had masses of the skins of the dappled antelope gleaming suspended from their boughs.

VIDÚSHAKA.

O friend, where now is all thy firmness gone?

JÍMÚTAVÁHANA.

Am I not firm beyond measure? What! have I not passed through the nights, though radiant with the moon?

* The Hindus imagined that light came from the eye, and lighted up any object gazed upon.

Do I not drink in the scent of the blue lotus? and endure the jasmine-scented evening winds? Hear I not the humming of the bees upon the lotus pond? That you should thus openly taunt me, saying, "He is wanting in firmness in difficulties." (*After considering.*) Or rather, it was not so wrongly said, my friend Átreya, for am I not really wanting in firmness, since I cannot bear even flowery arrows, shot by a bodiless archer, woman-hearted that I am! How then can I say to you, "I am firm?"

VIDÚSHAKA (*to himself*).

Since he confesses his want of firmness, he reveals how excessively troubled his heart must be. How shall I divert it? (*Aloud.*) O friend, how is it that, neglecting your parents, you have again come hither already?

JÍMÚTAVÁHANA.

It is a suitable question. To whom should I tell it, if not to you? This very day I had a dream. I saw yon loved one—(*pointing with a finger*)—seated on a moonstone seat in this sandal-creeper bower, in tears, as if reproaching me in some love quarrel. I wish, therefore, to spend the remainder of the day in this sandal-creeper bower, made pleasant by the late presence of the loved one, as seen in my dream. Come, then, we will go.

[*They walk about.*

GIRL (*after listening in trepidation*).

O lady, there is a noise like footsteps.

MALAYAVATÍ (*looking at herself, with agitation*).

Do not let any one, by seeing the state that I am in, suspect the secret of my heart. Rise then. We will conceal ourselves in this red aśoka tree, and just see who it is.

[*They do so.*

VIDÚSHAKA.

Here is the sandal-creeper bower. So come along. We will enter.

[*They enter.*

JÍMÚTAVÁHANA.

Even this sandal-creeper bower with its moonstone seat delights me not, abandoned as it is by the moon-faced one, like the face of night without its moonlight.

GIRL (*having peeped*).

Lady, I give you joy. Is not this the very person on whom your heart is set?

MALAYAVATÍ (*with joy and agitation, after looking*).

O girl, now that I have seen him, through my extreme agitation I cannot remain here so near him. Suppose he should see us! Come, we will go elsewhere. (*After going one step, longingly.*) How my feet tremble!

GIRL (*with a smile*).

O timid one! who can see you as you stand here? Do you forget the red aśoka tree? Let us then sit down, and remain here.

[*They do so.*

VIDÚSHAKA (*looking about*).

Here, my friend, is that very moonstone seat.

[*Hero sighs with tears.*

GIRL.

O lady, I think their talk is about a dream. Let us listen then attentively.

[*They both listen.*

VIDÚSHAKA (*touching him with his hand*).

My friend, do I not say, " Here is that moonstone seat ?"

JIMÚTAVÁHANA (*sighing, with a tear*).

It is well guessed. (*Pointing to it with his hand.*) This is that very moonstone seat on which I saw the loved one; her pale face reclined upon her left shoot-like hand, and her breast heaving with deep sobs. When I delayed to soothe her, her fit of anger passed away ; and her slightly-quivering lip and burst of tears betrayed the real state of her feelings. We will sit therefore on this moonstone seat.

[*They both sit down.*

MALAYAVATÍ (*after considering*).

Who now can she be whom he thus talks about ?

GIRL.

Just as we unobserved are looking at him, so I hope you too have not been seen by him.

MALAYAVATÍ.

It is possible. But then again, he is talking fondly about some one with whom he had a love quarrel.

GIRL.

Lady, do not have such a suspicion, but let us listen further.

VIDÚSHAKA (*to himself*).

This sort of talk pleases him, so I will continue it. (*Aloud.*) Friend, how then was this weeping one addressed by you?

JÍMÚTAVÁHANA.

She was thus addressed : " This moonstone seat, moistened with the water of tears, seems as if oozing with dew from the rising of thy moonface."

MALAYAVATÍ (*angrily*).

O Chaturiká ! what more than this need we hear? Come, then, we will go.

GIRL (*taking her by the hand*).

Lady, say not so. It is you alone whom he saw in his dream. His glance, resting on another, would find no pleasure.

MALAYAVATÍ.

My heart is not convinced. So we will just wait until the end of this conversation.

JÍMÚTAVÁHANA.

I know what I will do. I will draw her on this stone seat, and amuse myself by looking on her picture. Go, then, and fetch me some pieces of red arsenic from the mountain side.

VIDÚSHAKA.

Whatever your highness orders. (*Walking about, he picks up something, and returns to him.*) You asked for one colour; but I have brought you some pieces from which you may easily get the five colours.* Let your highness draw.

[*Gives him something.*

JÍMÚTAVÁHANA.

Well done, my friend. (*He takes it and draws upon the stone, with rapture.*) See, my friend, even the sight of this first outline of the beloved face gladdens me, as a digit of the new moon,—that face which is a very feast to the eyes, beautiful as its full unimpaired disc.

[*He continues drawing.*

VIDÚSHAKA (*looking on with curiosity*).

Though she is not in sight, her very form is depicted. Well, it is marvellous.

JÍMÚTAVÁHANA (*with a smile*).

O friend! the beloved is in my presence, brought before me by my wishes. If, as I continually see her, I draw her, where is the marvel?

MALAYAVATÍ (*with tears*).

O Chaturiká! I know well the end of this discourse. Come, then, we will go and look for Mitrávasu.

* *The five colours.*—The St Petersburg Dictionary, under "varna," gives a reference for these five colours to Kátyáyana's S'rauta-sútra, xxii. 9, 13, where they are described as—blue, yellow, red, brown, and variegated (?).

GIRL (*with despair, to herself*).

Her impatience is regardless even of her very life. (*Aloud.*) O lady! has not Manoharíká gone to him? Perhaps, then, your brother Mitrávasu is on his way here.

Then enters MITRÁVASU.

MITRÁVASU.

I am thus bidden by my father, "My child Mitrávasu, this Jímútaváhana, by living so near us, has been well observed; therefore he is a suitable son-in-law. Let, then, our child Malayavatí be given to him." As for myself, through my dependence on her affection, I suffer a variable state of feeling; for, on the one hand, this young man is the ornament of the race of Vidyádhara kings, is clever, approved by the good, unrivalled in beauty, endowed with valour, is wise and modest; but, on the other hand, he would readily give up his life, through pity, on behalf of any living creature. Thus, when yielding up my peerless sister to such an one, I feel both satisfaction and sorrow. I have heard that Jímútaváhana is in the sandal-creeper bower, adjoining the grove of Gaurí. This is that bower, so I will enter.

[*Enters.*

VIDÚSHAKA (*seeing him, with excitement*).

O friend! cover over with this plantain leaf, that girl you have just drawn in the picture. Here, surely, is Mitrávasu, the young prince of the Siddhas, just arrived. Perhaps he will see it.

[*The hero covers it with the plantain leaf.*

MITRÁVASU (*entering*).

Prince, Mitrávasu bows to you.

JÍMÚTAVÁHANA (*looking at him*).

Welcome to Mitrávasu.　Take a seat here.

GIRL.

O lady ! your brother, Mitrávasu, has arrived.

MALAYAVATÍ.

I am well pleased to hear it.

JÍMÚTAVÁHANA.

O Mitrávasu ! is Vísvávasu, the king of the Siddhas, well ?

MITRÁVASU.

He is well.　By the command of my father I am come into your presence.

JÍMÚTAVÁHANA.

What says his Highness ?

MALAYAVATÍ.

I will just hear what salutation has been sent by my father.

MITRÁVASU (*with tears*).

My father says, " I have a daughter, by name Malaya-vatí, who is, so to speak, the very life of all this race of Siddha-rájas.　She is presented by me to thee.　Let her be accepted."

GIRL (*smiling*).

O lady! why are you not angry now?

MALAYAVATÍ (*with a blush and smiling, standing with face bent down*).

Do not laugh, girl. Have you forgotten that his heart is set on another?

JÍMÚTAVÁHANA (*aside*).

My friend, we are fallen into a difficulty.

VIDÚSHAKA (*aside*).

Ah! I perceive. With the exception of *her*, your mind is not satisfied with any other. Let him, then, be dismissed with some civil speech or other.

MALAYAVATÍ (*angrily, to herself*).

Cruel one, who does not know what this means?

JÍMÚTAVÁHANA.

Who in the world would not desire so honourable an alliance as that with your Highness? But a mind set in one direction cannot be readily turned in another. So that I cannot accept her.

[*Heroine faints.*

GIRL.

Revive, my lady.

VIDÚSHAKA (*to Mitrávasu*).

Since he is altogether dependent on others, what is the use of questioning him? Go, then, to his parents and ask them.

c

MITRÁVASU (*to himself*).

It is well said. He will not disobey his parents. His father dwells here in the precinct of Gaurí. So I will go there, and cause Malayavatí to be accepted for him by his father.

[The heroine comes to herself.

MITRÁVASU.

Assuredly the prince knows best, who has refused us after we have opened our hearts.

MALAYAVATÍ (*laughing angrily*).

How! Mitrávasu still talks with him, though humbled by rejection!

[Exit Mitrávasu.

MALAYAVATÍ (*to herself, looking at herself with tears*).

What is the use of still supporting this body of mine, defiled by ill-fortune, filled with excessive woe! I will hang myself to yonder Asoka tree with this Atimukta creeper, and so put an end to my life. So it shall be. (*Aloud, with a meaningless smile.*) Girl, just see whether Mitrávasu has gone or not, so that I, too, may depart.

GIRL
(*having gone a few steps, and looking back: to herself*).

I see that she has some intention different to her words; so I will not go, but, concealed here, will see what she intends to do.

MALAYAVATÍ
(*looking all round, and taking the noose, with tears*).

O revered Gaurí! since your promise has not been

fulfilled in this world, you will contrive that I be not equally full of sorrow in another state of existence.

[*So speaking, she places the noose on her neck.*

GIRL (*running up with agitation*).

Help, your highness, help! Here is the princess trying to destroy herself by hanging.

JÍMÚTAVÁHANA (*rushing up with excitement*).

Where? Where is she?

GIRL.

Here, in this Aśoka tree.

JÍMÚTAVÁHANA (*looking joyfully*).

This is the very object of my passion.

[*He takes the heroine by the hand, and casts aside the noose.*

JÍMÚTAVÁHANA.

Assuredly no such attempt should be made. O lovely one! remove from the creeper this hand, which vies with it in beauty. How could that hand, which I do not consider strong enough even to gather flowers, grasp a noose to hang yourself with?

MALAYAVATÍ (*with agitation*).

Girl, who is this? (*Looking at him angrily, she wishes to cast off his hand.*) Loose me, let go my hand. Who are you to stop me? What! must you be sued even in death?

JÍMÚTAVÁHANA.

How should I release your guilty hand, which was caught in the very act of placing a noose on a neck fit only for strings of pearls ?

VIDÚSHAKA.

What could have been the cause of this determination of hers to die ?

GIRL.

Was it not this friend of yours ?

JÍMÚTAVÁHANA.

How ! *I* the cause of her death ? I do not understand.

VIDÚSHAKA.

O lady ! how do you mean ?

GIRL (*meaningly*).

It was that loved one, whoever she is, that was painted by your friend on the stone. My mistress took this determination in a fit of despair, saying to herself, "Through his devotion to that woman, I am not accepted, even when offered to him by Mitrávasu."

JÍMÚTAVÁHANA (*joyfully, to himself*).

How, then ! This is that Malayavatí, daughter of Visvávasu ! Yet, except from the ocean, how could there be the birth of a digit of the moon ?* Ah ! How I have been taken in by her !

* The moon is fabled to have been produced from the ocean when it was churned by the gods for ambrosia.

VIDÚSHAKA.

O lady! if this be so, my friend here is blameless. If you do not believe me, however, go yourself and look on the surface of the stone.

[*The heroine, with joy and modesty, looking at the hero, draws away her hand.*

JÍMÚTAVÁHANA (*with a smile*).

I will not release it, until you have seen the object of my passion, drawn on the stone.

[*All walk about.*

VIDÚSHAKA (*having taken off the plantain leaf*).

O lady! look. Behold the individual his heart is set on.

MALAYAVATÍ (*having looked at it, aside, smiling*).

O Chaturiká! it is as if my very self were drawn there.

GIRL (*looking at the picture and at the heroine*).

O lady! why do you say, "It is *as if* myself were drawn there"? So exact is the likeness, that I do not know whether it is a reflection of you cast on the stone, or a drawing.

MALAYAVATÍ (*with a smile*).

Girl, I am put to shame by him, showing me drawn in a picture.

VIDÚSKAKA.

Your Gándharva marriage* is now complete, so you may release her hand. Here comes some one in great haste.

[*The hero releases her.*

(*Then enters a* SERVANT GIRL.)

SERVANT GIRL (*joyfully*).

O lady! good luck to you. You are accepted by the parents of Jímútaváhana.

VIDÚSHAKA (*dancing about*).

He! he! The desires of my friend are fulfilled, or rather, I should say, of her highness Malayavatí; or still better, not so much of either of these, as (*gesticulating eating*) of me, the Brahman.

SERVANT GIRL (*addressing* MALAYAVATÍ).

I am bidden by the young king Mitrávasu, "This is the marriage day of Malayavatí; go therefore quickly, and fetch her." Come, then, let us go.

VIDÚSHAKA.

O daughter of a slave, how can my friend remain here, when you have taken her away?

---

* A gándharva marriage is one of the eight forms of marriage mentioned by Manu, Book III. It is formed by the parties themselves through mutual affection, without any previous family arrangement.

SERVANT GIRL.

Desist, base one. Hasten, hasten. It is full time for your bath.

[*The heroine, looking affectionately and with modesty at the hero, goes out with her attendants.*

HERALD (*reciting behind the scenes*).

Lending to Mount Malaya a splendour like that of Meru, by reason of the showers of scented powder,—and all at once having the beauty of the mild sunshine of early dawn, through the red-lead dust,—the Siddha-world announces, by the songs of nymphs, rendered delightful by the sounding of their jingling anklets of red gems, that the time for your marriage bathing has arrived, which brings completion of your wishes.

VIDÚSHAKA (*after hearing this*).

O friend! the time for bathing has come opportunely.

JÍMÚTAVÁHANA (*joyfully*).

If so, why do we stop here? Come on. We will salute my father, and go to the bath.

[*Exeunt omnes.*

END OF SECOND ACT OF THE NÁGÁNANDA.

ACT III.

Then enters intoxicated, his garments tumbled and stained, with a cup in his hand, a PARASITE, and a SLAVE, carrying a vessel of wine on his shoulder.

PARASITE.

These are the only two gods for me—the one who is always drinking, and the one who brings lovers together —Baladeva * and Káma-deva. (*Reels about.*) Assuredly the life of me, S'ekharaka, is very prosperous, since in my bosom is a loved lady, in my mouth lotus-scented wine, and on my head a garland, like a perpetual minister to my wants. (*Stumbles.*) Halloa! Who is pushing against me now? (*With joy.*) Assuredly Navamáliká makes game of me.

SLAVE.

She is not yet come, sir.

PARASITE (*angrily*).

The marriage of Malayavatí took place in the first watch; how, then, is she not come yet, though it is morning? (*Thinking for a time, with joy.*) I suppose that at the marriage feast all the Siddha and Vidyádhara people, with their friends and acquaintances, are enjoying the delight of drinking in the flower-garden; so that there Navamáliká will be looking out for me. So

---

* Baladeva, the elder brother of Krishna, celebrated for his drinking exploits; a sort of Bacchus.

I will now go there. What is S'ekharaka without Navamálikâ ?*

[*He begins to go out, staggering.*

SLAVE.

Come along, sir. Here is the flower-garden. Be pleased to enter.

Then enters the VIDÚSHAKA, *with a pair of garments on his shoulder.*

VIDÚSHAKA.

The desires of my dear friend are fulfilled. I am told that he is on his way to the flower-garden. So I will now go there. (*Walking and looking about.*) Here is the flower-garden. I will enter. (*After entering, gesticulating as if annoyed by bees.*) Halloa ! Why now do these odious bees attack me ? (*Smelling himself.*) Ah ! I see how it is. I have been respectfully decked with perfumes by the relations of Malayavatí, as the bridegroom's friend, and a garland of Santána flowers has been placed upon my head, and now that very respect has become a cause of annoyance. What shall I do ? Having dressed myself as a woman with these pieces of red cloth, which I have brought from Malayavatí, I will go on, using the upper garment as a veil. We will see what these villanous bees will then do.

[*He does so.*

PARASITE (*observing him, joyfully*).

Halloa! slave. (*Pointing laughingly with his finger.*)

* Both these names are significant. S'ekharaka properly means a garland, and Navamálikâ the double-jasmine.

Here is surely Navamáliká.   She has seen me, and, in
a rage at my long delay, puts on her veil and turns
away.   So I will appease her with caresses.

[*Going up, with a laugh, and embracing the* VIDÚSHAKA,
he tries to put some betel nut in his mouth.

VIDÚSHAKA (*perceiving the smell of wine, holds his nose,
and turns away his face*).

How now ?   Having but just escaped the attack of
bees of one sort, I am assailed by an odious bee of a
different nature.*

PARASITE.

Why do you turn away your face in anger ?   (*Prostrat-
ing himself, and placing the* VIDÚSHAKA'S *foot on his head.*)
Be appeased, O Navamáliká !

Then enters a SERVANT GIRL.

GIRL.

I am bidden by the queen—" O Navamáliká, go to the
flower-garden, and say to the keeper, Pallaviká, ' To-day,
prepare the tamála-bower with especial care, for the
bridegroom and Malayavatí are going thither.' "   I have
given the message to Pallaviká ; and I will now seek my
dear friend, S'ekharaka, whose passion will be increased
by my night's absence.   (*Seeing him.*)   Here he is.
(*Angrily.*)   How now !   He is courting some other
woman !   I will just stop, and find out who she is.

* A pun on the word " madhukara," which means both a " bee "
and a " lover."

PARASITE (*joyfully*).

He who, through excessive pride, bows not to S'iva,
Vishnu, or Brahma, that same S'ekharaka falls at thy
feet, O Navamáliká.

VIDÚSHAKA.

Oh drunken wretch, there is no Navamáliká here.

GIRL (*looking, with a smile*).

S'ekharaka, overcome with wine, is soothing his
reverence Átreya in mistake for me. I will put on a
pretence of anger, and have a game with them.

SLAVE (*having seen the SERVANT GIRL, shaking S'EK-
HARAKA with his hand*).

Sir, let her go. It is not Navamáliká. Here is
Navamáliká, just come, and looking on, with eyes lit up
with anger.

GIRL (*going up*).

Well, S'ekharaka, whom are you courting here ?

VIDÚSHAKA (*letting the veil drop*).

O lady, it is only I, an ill-fated Brahman.

PARASITE (*recognising the VIDÚSHAKA*).

Halloa ! You tawny monkey, would you too deceive
S'ekharaka ? Come, slave, take hold of him, whilst I
soothe Navamáliká.

SLAVE.

Whatever my master orders.

PARASITE (*letting go the* VIDÚSHAKA, *and falling at the feet of the* SERVANT GIRL).

Be be appeased, appeased, O Navamáliká!

VIDÚSHAKA (*to himself*).

This seems a good opportunity to make off.

> [*Tries to get away.*

SLAVE (*grasping the* VIDÚSHAKA *by his Brahmanical cord, which is broken in the struggle*).

·Where are you off to, you tawny monkey?

> [*Binding him round the neck by the upper garment, he drags him along.*

VIDÚSHAKA.

O lady, Navamáliká, be appeased.   Make him release me.

GIRL.

If you fall at my feet, with your head on the ground.

> [*She laughs.*

VIDÚSHAKA (*with anger, and trembling*).

Alas!   How can I, who am a Brahman, and friend of the king of the Gandharvas, fall at the feet of the daughter of a slave?

GIRL (*shaking her finger at him, and smiling*).

I will compel you to bow presently.—Get up, S'ekharaka, get up.   I am satisfied.   (*She embraces him.*) But here the dear friend of the bridegroom has been insulted by you, and I daresay your master, Mitrávasu, will be angry on hearing of it. So you had better pay respect to him.

PARASITE.

Whatsoever Navamáliká orders. (*After embracing the* VIDÚSHAKA.) O sir, you were joked with by me, thinking you were one of my relations. (*Reeling about.*) Am I really Sekharaka? Has any joke really been made? (*Making his upper garment into a bundle, he offers it as a seat.*) Let my relation take a seat here.

VIDÚSHAKA (*to himself*).

Thank goodness! he has passed the violent stage of his drunkenness.

[*He sits down.*

PARASITE.

O Navamáliká, do you take a seat at his side, so that I may pay my respects to you both at once.

[SERVANT GIRL, *with a laugh, sits down.*

PARASITE (*taking up the drinking-cup*).

Slave, fill this to the brim with wine.

[SLAVE *gesticulates the filling of the cup.*

PARASITE (*taking some flowers from the garland on his head, puts them into the cup, and kneeling on both knees, presents it to* NAVAMÁLIKÁ).

O Navamáliká, taste it, and pass it to him.

GIRL (*with a smile*).

Whatever you wish.

[*Tastes, and gives it back.* `

PARASITE

(*presenting the cup to the* VIDÚSHAKA).

This cup, with its contents specially flavoured by contact with the lips of Navamálika, has never before been
tasted, except by S'ekharaka.   Drink, therefore.   What
greater honour could I show you?

VIDÚSHAKÁ (*with a very forced smile*).

O S'ekharaka, I am a Brahman.

PARASITE.

If so, where is your ninefold thread?*

VIDÚSHAKA.

It was dragged and broken by that slave.

GIRL (*laughingly*).

Recite to us, then, some verses of the Vedas.

VIDÚSHAKA.

O lady, what have the smell of wine and verses of the
Vedas in common?†   However, I have no wish to argue
with you.   The Brahman falls at your feet.

[*Offers to fall at her feet.*

* See Manu II. 44, Comm.
† In Manu IV. 3, a priest is forbidden to pronounce texts of the
Veda, "as long as the scent and unctuosity of perfumes remain on
his body" after an entertainment.

GIRL (*checking him with both hands*).

Your reverence must not do so. O S'ekharaka, get away, get away; he is really a Brahman.* (*She falls at the feet of the* VIDÚSHAKA.) O sir, do not nurse your wrath. This was only a piece of friendly joking.

PARASITE (*to himself*).

I too had better appease him. (*Falling at his feet, aloud.*) Let your reverence forgive me for having offended under the influence of wine. I will now go with Navamáliká to the drinking-booth.

VIDUSHAKA.

I forgive you. Be off, both of you. I too will go and see my dear patron.

[*Exeunt* PARASITE, *with* SLAVE, *and* SERVANT GIRL.

VIDÚSHAKA.

The untimely death of a Brahman has been averted. But since I am defiled by contact with this drunken youth, I will just bathe in this tank. (*He does so. Looking towards the tiring-room.*) Here comes my dear friend, supporting Malayavatí, like Krishna supporting Rukminí.† I will go and attend upon them.

Then enters the hero, dressed in marriage garments, with MALAYAVATÍ, *and a suitable retinue.*

JÍMÚTAVÁHANA

(*looking, with rapture, at* MALAYAVATÍ).

When looked upon, she casts down her eye; when

* See Manu XI. 206.

† Rukminí was the chief wife of Krishna. See Prem Ságar, ch. lxxxiii.

addressed, she makes no reply; on the couch, she remains turned away; when excessively embraced, she trembles; when her friends leave the room, she too wishes to go out: through the very perversity of her behaviour my newly-married love is still more to my liking. (*Looking at* MALAYAVATÍ.) O beloved Malayavatí, a vow of silence was kept by me, though accustomed to answer in haughty tones; this body of mine was bathed in the rays of the sun and moon, and in the flames of forest fires; and I was rapt in total abstraction of mind for many days and nights. Surely the fruit of all that penance is, that I now behold this face of thine.

MALAYAVATÍ (*aside*).

O Chaturiká, he is not only pleasant to the eye, but he knows also how to speak in a flattering manner.

GIRL (*smiling*).

You might say so, if he *was* flattering. But where is the flattery in this?

JÍMÚTAVÁHANA.

O Chaturiká, point out the path to the flower-garden.

GIRL.

This way, my lord.

JÍMÚTAVÁHANA
(*walking about, addressing the heroine*).

Let your ladyship come just as you are. The weight of your breasts themselves tends to weary you; why, then place a pearl ornament on your waist? The weight of your hips is wearisome,—much more this girdle! There is hardly sufficient power in your feet to carry your limbs, far less your anklets! Your limbs being so lovely, why should you wear ornaments that only tend to weary you?

GIRL.

Here is the flower-garden. Be pleased to enter.

[*All enter.*

JÍMÚTAVÁHANA (*looking round*).

Well, truly the beauty of the flower-garden is great! Here the droppings from the sandal-trees cool the creeper-bower with its tesselated pavement. The peacock dances yet more wildly to the shrill sound of the shower-baths. The cascade, brown with the pollen of flowers, shaken from the trees by the impetuous foam, falls with a rush from the machine, and fills the basins at the foot of the trees. Again, these bees, making the creeper-bower resound with their attempts at song, as they drink in abundant honey, in company with their wives, covered with a perfumed dust by the pollen of flowers, seem to enjoy on every side a drinking festival.

[VIDÚSHAKA *comes up.*

VIDÚSHAKA.

Victory to your highness! Welcome to your ladyship!

JÍMÚTAVÁHANA.

O friend! you have been very long in coming.

D

VIDÚSHAKA.

I am come as soon as I could. But I delayed so long walking about, through curiosity to see the drinking of the Vidyádharas and Siddhas, intermingled at the marriage feast. Do you, too, just take a look at them.

JÍMÚTAVÁHANA.

We will do as you say. (*Looking on all sides.*) Friend, see, see! Their limbs anointed with yellow sandal, and wearing wreaths of Santána flowers, with their bright garments variegated by the mixture of rays from their jewelled ornaments, these Vidyádharas and Siddhas, intermingled beneath the shade of the sandal-trees, drink the nectar, just tasted and left by their loved ones. Come, we will go to the tamála avenue.

[*Walks about.*

VIDÚSHAKA.

Here is the tamála avenue. Her ladyship appears fatigued with walking to it. Let us therefore sit down on this crystal seat, and rest.

JÍMÚTAVÁHANA.

Friend, it is well suggested. The face of my dear one, after having worsted the moon by the pale beauty of its cheeks, now surely wishes to surpass the lotus when reddened by the sun's rays. (*Taking the heroine by the hand.*) Dear one, let us sit down.

MALAYAVATÍ.

Whatever my husband bids me.

[*All sit down.*

JÍMÚTAVÁHANA.

(raising the heroine's face, and looking at it).

Dear one, to no purpose hast thou been wearied by us, through our anxiety to see the flower garden, since this face of thine, resplendent with its creepers of eyebrows and shoot-like pink lips, is a very garden of paradise. Compared with this, every garden is but a jungle.

GIRL *(addressing the* VIDÚSHAKA, *with a smile).*

You have heard how he describes the princess. I will now paint you.

VIDÚSHAKA *(gladly).*

O lady! I am alive again now. Pray, then, do me the favour in your best style, that yon fellow may never again call me a tawny monkey.

GIRL.

Sir, you seemed lovely to me at the marriage watch, with your eyes shut through drowsiness. Therefore stand like that for me to paint you.

[VIDÚSHAKA *does so.*

GIRL *(to herself).*

Whilst he stands with his eyes shut, I will blacken his face with the juice of a tamála shoot, which will do as well as indigo.

[*Rising and squeezing a tamála shoot,
she blackens his face.*

(*The hero and heroine look at the* VIDÚSHAKA.)

JÍMÚTAVÁHANA.

Friend, you are in luck, being painted, with us for spectators.

[*Heroine laughs on seeing* VIDÚSHAKA'S *face.*

JÍMÚTAVÁHANA (*looking in her face*).

O lovely-eyed one! the springing of the *blossom* of a smile is seen on your shoot-like lower lip, but the *fruit* is seen elsewhere, namely, in the eyes of me as I gaze.

VIDÚSHAKA.

Madam, what have you done?

GIRL.

Why, are you not painted?

VIDÚSHAKA (*after rubbing his hand over his face and looking at it, raising his staff*).

O daughter of a slave! the royal family are present. What shall I do to you?—Alas! notwithstanding your royal presence, I am blackened by this daughter of a slave. How can I remain here? I will be off.

[*Exit.*

GIRL.

His reverence Átreya is vexed with me. I will go and conciliate him.

MALAYAVATÍ.

O Chaturiká! whither do you go, leaving me all alone?

GIRL (*pointing to the hero, and smiling*).

May you be long in such solitude !

[*Exit.*

JÍMÚTAVÁHANA (*looking in the face of heroine*).

O lovely one ! if this face of thine, with its pink flush as it is lighted up by the sun's rays, and with its soft down revealed by the spreading gleam of its teeth, is really a lotus, why is not a bee seen drinking the honey from it ?*

(*Heroine, laughing, turns her face another way.*)

(*Hero repeats the same sentence.*)

GIRL

(*entering with a hurried toss of the curtain, and coming up*).

Here is the noble Mitrávasu, desirous to see the prince on some business.

JÍMÚTAVÁHANA.

Dear one, do you go to the house. I too will soon come, after I have seen Mitrávasu.

[*Exit heroine with servant girl.*

Then enters MITRÁVASU.

MITRÁVASU.

Whilst that enemy is still unslain, how can I without a sense of shame say to Jímútaváhana, "Your kingdom is seized by an enemy?" Still, it is not right to go without informing him. So I will tell him and then go. O prince ! Mitrávasu salutes you.

* A polite way of asking for a kiss. See note on p. 42.

JÍMÚTAVÁHANA (*on seeing* MITRÁVASU).

Pray, be seated.

[MITRÁVASU *takes a seat, keeping his eyes fixed on him.*

JÍMÚTAVÁHANA (*looking steadily at him*).

O Mitrávasu! you seem vexed.

MITRÁVASU.

Who would be put out by one so despicable as Matanga?

JÍMÚTAVÁHANA.

What has Matanga been doing?

MITRÁVASU.

Assuredly to his own destruction, he has attacked your kingdom.

JÍMÚTAVÁHANA (*with joy, to himself*).

Oh! would that it were true!

MITRÁVASU.

Therefore let the prince deign to give orders for his destruction. What need of talking long about it? As soon as, at thy command, the Siddhas are gone hence to battle, making the day dark by clouding the sun, as if it were the rainy season, with their heaven-traversing chariots crowding on every side,—your monarchy, whose zemindars are temporarily bowing through fear of this haughty enemy, will at once be regained. What need though of great multitudes? By me, single-handed, shining with an aureole of rays from the quickly-drawn sword, behold the coward Matanga already slain on the battle-field, like a mighty elephant by a lion which has sprung on him from afar.

JÍMÚTAVÁHANA (*to himself, covering his ears*).

Ah! how cruelly he speaks! However, let it pass. (*Aloud.*) O Mitrávasu! what is all this? Even something more than this might be possible for you, with such strong arms. But how should I, a man who through pity, though unasked, would give up his own body for the sake of another, permit the cruelty of destroying life for the sake of a kingdom? For my part, I can conceive no enemy except the Kleśas.* If, then, you would please me, pity that poor wretch, who, for the sake of kingly power, has become a slave to the Kleśas.

MITRÁVASU (*bitterly*).

One, forsooth, who has done so much good to us, and is in such misfortune, is well worthy of pity!

JÍMÚTAVÁHANA (*to himself*).

His wrath is not to be averted. His mind, swayed by passion, cannot be turned aside. Well, let it be. (*Aloud.*) Rise, we will go in-doors. There I will advise you. The day is now ended,—for yonder sun, the sole object worthy of adulation, whose favour is solely for

---

* *Kleśas.*—The kleśas are well known in Buddhist theology. See Burnouf, "Lotus de la bonne loi," App. II. They are the ten vices, thus divided :—Three of the body, murder, theft, adultery; four of speech, lying, slander, abuse, unprofitable conversation; three of the mind, covetousness, malice, scepticism. In the Yoga philosophy there are five : ignorance, egotism, desire, hatred, tenacity of existence.

the good of others, is looked on by the Siddhas, with
their voices loud in continual praise, as he goes to rest,
having vivified the universe with his rays, whose sole
business is to fill the eight quarters with light, and to
keep off from the lotus buds the binding seal of sleep.

[*Exeunt omnes.*

END OF THE THIRD ACT.

ACT IV.

Then enter a CHAMBERLAIN *carrying two red garments,
and a* DOORKEEPER.

CHAMBERLAIN.

I, who issue commands for the seraglio, who watch
for trippings at every step, now, weak through old age,
make my resemblance to a king perfect by handling a
" da*nda*." *

DOORKEEPER.

O reverend Vasubhadra ! whither are you going ?

CHAMBERLAIN.

I am bidden by the queen, the mother of Mitrávasu : "O
chamberlain ! for ten days you should take red garments
to Malayavatí and my son-in-law." Now the daughter
is remaining in her father-in-law's household, and Jímútaváhana is gone to-day with the young king to see the

* We have here a pun, as the word da*nda*-níti means both " pun-
ishment and policy " and " the handling of a staff."

sea-shore, as I have heard. Whether, then, shall I go to the king's daughter or to the son-in-law?

DOORKEEPER.

Sir, you had better go to the princess, for perhaps by this time the son-in-law will have come there of his own accord.

CHAMBERLAIN.

You advise well. But whither are you yourself now going?

DOORKEEPER.

I am commissioned by King Viśvávasu to go and tell Mitrávasu, "Since in this festival of 'Dípa-pratipad'* some present should be given to Malayavatí and the bridegroom, therefore come and think of something suitable to the occasion."

[*Exeunt both.*

Then enter JÍMÚTAVÁHANA *and* MITRÁVASU.

JÍMÚTAVÁHANA.

A green glade for a couch, a white stone for a seat, a dwelling beneath the trees, the cool water of a cascade for drink, roots for food, the deer for companions,—in the forest which thus abounds in all that one could wish, unsought, there is this one fault, that, through the absence of suppliants, we live there to no purpose, having no opportunity of assisting others.

* " Dípa-pratipad " may mean the first day of the bright fortnight, or perhaps a festival corresponding to the Feast of Lauterns.

MITRÁVASU (*looking upwards*).

Prince, hasten, hasten! It is time for the flow of the
tide.

JÍMÚTAVÁHANA (*listening*).

You are right. An ear-deafening noise arises, made
by the repeated flappings of the ears of the sea-monsters
as they emerge, and causing the interiors of all the
mountain caves to re-echo. Here comes the tide, white
with the innumerable shells which it tosses on its waves.

MITRÁVASU.

It is indeed come. See! this ocean tide is brilliant
with its many-coloured gems, and has its waters scented
by the eructations of the sea-monsters, who have fed on
the young shoots of the clove-trees.*

JÍMÚTAVÁHANA.

O Mitrávasu! see again. These slopes of Malaya have
all the splendour of the peaks of the snow mountains,
by reason of the veils of white autumnal clouds.

MITRÁVASU.

These are not the slopes of Malaya. These are heaps
of the bones of Nágas.

JÍMÚTAVÁHANA (*sorrowfully*).

Alas! wherefore were they thus slain by wholesale?

---

* Compare the passage in Indumatí's Swayamvara, Raghuvanśa,
vi. 57, where Sunandá recommends the princess to choose the King
of Kalinga or Coromandel: "Wander with him on the banks of the
ocean, resonant with the murmurs of the palm groves, while the
summer heat is cooled by the breezes which bear the flowers of the
clove-tree, wafted from other lands,"

MITRÁVASU.

They were not slain by wholesale. Just listen to this: At this place Garuda* was in the habit of devouring one snake daily, catching it up from hell, whilst the whole contents of the ocean were cleft asunder from top to bottom by the wind of his wings.

JÍMÚTAVÁHANA (*in a mournful tone*).

Alas! his deed was most cruel. And then?

MITRÁVASU.

Then Garuda was addressed by Vásuki,† who feared annihilation of the whole serpent race——

JÍMÚTAVÁHANA (*with respect*).

Did he say, "Eat me first"?

MITRÁVASU.

No, no.

JÍMÚTAVÁHANA.

What then?

MITRÁVASU.

This is what he said: " Through fear of your furious descent, the embryos of the snakes are prematurely born by thousands, and the young ones perish; so that our continuous line of descent is cut off, and your own interests are destroyed. Therefore that snake, for the

* Garuda, son of Vinatá and Kaśyapa, is the king of birds, like the fabled roc, and the ruthless enemy of the snakes or Nágas.

† Vásuki is king of the Nágas, and resides in the infernal regions.

sake of which you make your descent into hell, I will send to you daily to this place."

JÍMÚTAVÁHANA.

How well were the snakes defended by their king! Amidst his thousand double tongues was there not one with which he could say, " Myself is given by me this day to save the life of a snake."

MITRÁVASU.

This, then, was agreed to by the king of birds. So, these conditions being thus settled by the king of the Nágas, these are the heaps, white as the snow peaks, from the bones of the snakes, which the king of birds devours, and which have been increasing, do increase, and will increase as days go by.

JÍMÚTAVÁHANA.

Wonderful! Fools commit sin even for the sake of a worthless body, which soon perishes, is ungrateful, and is a store-house of all uncleanness. Well, this destruction of the Nágas will assuredly bring some judgment. (*To himself.*) Would that, by giving up my own body, I might save the life of a single Nága!

Then enters the DOORKEEPER.

DOORKEEPER.

I have ascended the mountain peak and will now seek Mitrávasu. (*Walking about.*) Here stands Mitrávasu with the bridegroom. (*Going up.*) May the princes be victorious!

MITRÁVASU.

O Sunanda, why are you come? *(Doorkeeper whispers in his ear.)* O prince, my father has sent for me.

JÍMÚTAVÁHANA.

Go, then.

MITRÁVASU.

The prince should not stay too long in this ill-omened region.

[Exit.

JÍMÚTAVÁHANA.

I will descend from this mountain peak and look at the sea-shore. *(Walks about.)*

Behind the scenes.

Alas! my darling son, S'ankhachúda, how can I endure to see thee slain to-day?

JÍMÚTAVÁHANA *(after hearing this).*

Ha! a cry of distress as if from a woman! Who can it be? of what is she afraid? I will try to know.

[Walks about.

Then enters S'ANKHACHÚDA, *followed by an* OLD WOMAN, *crying, and a* SERVANT *with a pair of garments for one completely veiled.*

OLD WOMAN *(with tears).*

Alas! my son, S'ankhachúda, how can I endure to see you slain this day? *(Taking hold of his chin.*)* Deprived of this moonface, Hades will become midnight.

---

* The Nágas are generally represented in old sculptures as bearing the human form, but with a snake attached to their backs and the hooded head rising behind their necks.

S'ANKHACHÚDA.

O mother, why do you harass me yet more by weeping?

OLD WOMAN (*looking at him and stroking his limbs*).

Alas! my son! how will pitiless Garuda devour thy beauteous body, that has never felt the sun's rays?

[*Embracing him, she weeps.*

S'ANKHACHÚDA.

Enough of lamentation. See here—since mortality as the nurse first clasps the new-born child to its bosom, and the mother comes only second—what room is there for sorrow?

[*Wishes to depart.*

OLD WOMAN.

O son, stay for a moment whilst I look on your face.

SERVANT.

Come, Prince S'ankhachúda, never mind her words. Infatuated by affection for her son, she forgets the duty to our king.

S'ANKHACHÚDA.

I am coming.

SERVANT (*to himself, looking in advance*).

I have brought him to the rock of execution; so I will now give him the distinguishing badge of one condemned to death.

JÍMÚTAVÁHANA.

This must be the woman that I heard—(*looking at Sankhachúda*)—and this must be her son. Why, then, does she weep? (*Looks on all sides.*) I do not perceive the very least cause for her fear. I will go near and see whence her fear is. Their conversation relates to it, perhaps from it I may get some explanation. I will get inside a bush and listen.

SERVANT (*with tears, putting his hands together*).

O Prince S'ankhachúda, since it is the command of my lord, this so cruel message must be delivered.

S'ANKHACHÚDA.

Say on.

SERVANT.

The king of the Nágas orders——

S'ANKHACHÚDA.

(*putting his hands together to his head, respectfully*). What does our lord order?

SERVANT.

"Having put on this pair of red garments, mount upon the rock of execution, that Garuda, on seeing the red garments, may eat you."

JÍMÚTAVÁHANA (*having overheard*).

How! Is he, then, abandoned by Vásuki?

SERVANT.

O prince, take then this pair of garments.

[*Presents them.*

S'ANKHACHÚDA (*respectfully*).

Give them to me. (*Takes them.*) The mandate of our lord is on my head.

OLD WOMAN (*having seen the clothes in the hand of her son, striking her breast*).

Alas! my child, this seems like a flash of lightning.

[*Faints.*

SERVANT.

The time for Garuda's approach is close at hand. I will be off.

[*Exit.*

S'ANKHACHÚDA.

O mother, recover thyself.

OLD WOMAN (*coming to herself, tearfully*).

Alas! my son, alas! thou obtained by a hundred vows! Where shall I again behold thee?

[*She clasps him round the neck.*

JÍMÚTAVÁHANA.

Alas! the pitilessness of Garuda. I should think that the heart of the lord of birds must be made of very adamant, if, casting away all pity, he can eat this child in his mother's lap, while she, distracted, utters vain complaints, with tears streaming from her eyes, and, glancing in all directions, pitifully repeats—" My child, who will deliver thee ?"

S'ANKHACHÚ*DA* (*checking his own tears*).

O mother, where is the use of excessive grief? Do I not keep saying, " Cheer up," " Cheer up ?"

OLD WOMAN (*with tears*).

How can I cheer up, seeing that thou, my son, my only son, art banished by the compassionate king of the Nágas ! Alas? why in the universal world was *my* son thought of? I am utterly unfortunate.

[*She faints.*

JÍMÚTAVÁHANA (*dolefully*).

If I do not protect this wretched one, who is at the very point of death, abandoned by his relations, then what good is there in my body? So I will go up to them.

S'ANKHACHÚ*DA*.

O mother, be comforted.

OLD WOMAN.

Alas ! my son, when you are given up by Vásuki, the protector of the Nága-world, who else will be your protector ?

JÍMÚTAVÁHANA (*going up*).

Shall not *I?*

OLD WOMAN (*on seeing him, having hid her son with her upper garment, goes up to him and falls upon her knees*).

O son of Vinatá, destroy me. I am prepared for thy food by the Nága king.

E

JÍMÚTAVÁHANA (*with tears*).

Alas! the love of offspring! I should think that after seeing this sorrow of hers, arising from affection for her son, even the enemy of the Nágas, whose heart is pitiless, will feel pity.

SANKHACHÚDA.

O mother, away with your fear, this is not the enemy of the Nágas. See the difference between this holy one, whose appearance indicates a beauteous nature, and Garuda, with his fierce beak smeared with clots of blood, which have dropped whilst he was piercing the brains of the mighty Nágas.

OLD WOMAN.

In truth, through fear of thy death, I regard this whole world as Garuda.

JÍMÚTAVÁHANA.

O mother, what need of saying it again and again? Will not I accomplish his deliverance?

OLD WOMAN (*clasping her hands on her head*).

My son, live long!

JÍMÚTAVÁHANA.

Mother, give me this distinguishing badge of a condemned one. I will put it on and offer to the son of Vinatá my own body as food, to save the life of thy son.

OLD WOMAN (*stopping her ears*).

God forbid! Thou also art a son equally with Sankhachúda, or even more so than he, since thou wishest to preserve my son by giving up thy own body, even though he is deserted by his own kinsfolk.

S'ANKHACHÚDA.

How different from the world in general is the mind of this magnanimous one! For this good man, moved by pity, gives up for the sake of another as though it were but a straw, that life, for the sake of which, in olden times, Viśvámitra * ate dog's flesh, like a dog-cooker; and Nádijangha † was slain by Gautama, even though he had done a kindness to him; and this Garuda, son of Kaśyapa, daily eats Nágas. *(Addressing the hero.)* O magnanimous one, unfeigned compassion for me has been fully shown by thee in the determination to give up thyself; but do not obstinately insist on it. Low-born people like me are born and die; but whence are those produced like thee, who gird up their loins for the sake of others? What, then, is the use of this fixed determination? Let this resolution be abandoned.

JÍMÚTAVÁHANA.

O S'ankhachúda, do not put any obstacle in the way of this desire of mine of giving myself up for the sake of another, which only now has got an opportunity of accomplishment, after so long a time. Do not, then, hesitate, but give me the distinctive badge of those appointed to be slain.

---

* Compare Manu x. 108, "And Viśvámitra, who knew right and wrong, resolved to eat a dog's thigh, taking it from the hand of a chandála."

† For the story of Nádijangha, see Maháb. xii. §§ 170-172.

S'ANKHACHÚDA.

O magnanimous one, where is the use of this fruitless perseverance? Never will S'ankhachúda sully the family honour of S'ankhapála, which is white as a shell. If we are indeed objects worthy of thy pity, then let some expedient be devised, so that this woman may not quit life, overcome by my calamity.

JÍMÚTAVÁHANA.

What can possibly be devised? She who dies in your death and lives only in your life,—if you wish her to live, save yourself by my life. This is the only remedy, so give me quickly the badge of death, that, having disguised myself in it, I may mount the execution rock. And do you, thinking of your mother before all, retire from your post. Probably your mother, if she stood in view of the place of execution, would abandon life. Do you not see the great cemetery, filled with many skeletons of the ill-fated Nágas? See here, rows upon rows of the crests of the slain Nágas, coated thick with oozing brains, splash as they fall from the jaws of the jackalls into the stream of carrion-smelling gore, while the scene is shrouded in awful darkness by the flapping wings of the vultures, their greed increased by the gobbets of raw flesh which fall mangled from their chattering beaks!

S'ANKHACHÚDA.

How should I not see? This cemetery, which affords delight to Garuda, with a snake for his daily food, is like the body of S'iva, with its skulls and bones white as the moon.*

JÍMÚTAVÁHANA.

O S'ankhachúda, go then. What is the use of these well-meant objections ?

S'ANKHACHÚDA.

The time for the approach of Garuḍa is close at hand. (*Goes on his knees before his mother.*) O mother, do you now go away. In whatever state we may be born again, mayst thou alone be my mother, O doting one !

[*Falls at her feet.*

OLD WOMAN (*with tears.*)

How ! Is this the very last speech ? O son, my feet assuredly will not bear me from thee, therefore I will stay here.

S'ANKHACHÚDA (*rising*).

After I have quickly walked round the southern Gokarṇa,† which is close at hand, I will carry out the command of my lord.

[*Exeunt both.*

JÍMÚTAVÁHANA.

(*having seen some one coming, joyfully, to himself*).

Good luck ! I have got what I wanted, through the unexpected acquisition of this pair of red garments.

---

* S'iva is often represented as wearing an elephant's skin and a necklace of skulls.

† Gokarna—there are two celebrated places of pilgrimage called Gokarna,—the northern one in Nepal, the southern on the Malabar coast. See Wilson's " Essays on the Religion of the Hindus," ii. 16, 19. The manner of " walking round " was, to keep the right shoulder always towards the sacred place.

CHAMBERLAIN (*entering*).

This pair of garments is sent by the Queen, the mother of Mitrávasu, to the prince. Let, then, the prince put them on.

JÍMÚTAVÁHANA (*with respect*).

Give them to me. (*Chamberlain gives them,—to himself*). My marriage with Malayavatí has borne good fruit. (*Aloud.*) You may depart. Let the Queen be saluted from me.

CHAMBERLAIN.

Whatever your highness orders.

[*Exit.*

JÍMÚTAVÁHANA.

The seasonable arrival of this pair of red garments gives me the greatest pleasure, inasmuch as I desire to give myself up for another. (*Looking in all directions.*) From the violence of this wind, which shakes the mighty rocks of the Malayan peaks, I suspect that the king of birds is now close at hand. See, the expanse of his wings obscures the sky, like the clouds at doomsday; the wind caused by his rush casts the waters of ocean on the shore, as if for another deluge; and,—raising an apprehension of the sudden ending of the world, and watched with terror by the elephants that support the earth,—with the refulgence of his body, which shines like the twelve suns,* he spreads a lurid red gleam over the ten

---

* Twelve suns or Ádityas. These twelve Ádityas are forms of the sun, who, according to the later mythology of the Hindus, had a different form for each month.

quarters of the sky. Therefore now, while S'ankhachúda is away, I will quickly mount the execution rock. (*Does so and sits down, starting as if enraptured.*) Oh, the rapture of its touch! Not so much does Malayavatí delight me, moist with sandal-juice of Malaya, as this rock of execution, which I embrace to the furtherance of my desired object. Or rather—what need of mentioning Malayavatí? Not such joy is attained by one in childhood, lying peacefully in his mother's lap, as by me on the slope of this rock of execution. Here comes Garuḍa. I must veil myself.

[*Does so.*

Then enters GARUḌA.

GARUḌA.

Here I am, in a moment arrived on the shore side of the Malayan Mount, greedy to devour the Nága. When I saw the moon's disk, I was reminded of the form of S'esha* coiled up in a circle through fear. My elder brother † joyfully recognised me, when the sun was shaken by the sudden start of his chariot steeds as I passed. My long wings, as I fly, stretch out still longer by reason of the clouds, that hang from them in festoons.

JÍMÚTAVÁHANA (*with joy*).

Through the merit that I gain to-day, by protecting a Nága at the sacrifice of myself, may I still obtain,

---

* S'esha is the thousand-headed snake which serves Vishnu as his couch and canopy.

† Aruṇa, who is the personified dawn, and charioteer of the sun.

in succeeding existences, a body to be sacrificed for others !*

GARUDA (*looking at the hero*).

Speedily will I catch up and eat this Nága, dressed in red garments, who looks as if besmeared with blood, which gushes from his heart that has burst through fear of me. I will first split open with my beak, which is fiercer than the fierceness of a thunderbolt, the breast of this one, who has fallen on the surface of the execution rock, to save the rest of Nágas.

[*Making a descent, he seizes the hero.*

Behind the scenes flowers shower down, and drums sound.

GARUDA (*astonished*).

Why now does this shower of flowers fall, rejoicing the bees with their fragrance ? Or why does this noise of drums cause to re-echo the quarters of the sky ? (*Smiling.*) Ah! I know what it is. I conjecture that even the tree of Paradise itself is shaken by the wind of my speed ; and that the clouds of doomsday give forth their growl, anticipating the world's immediate annihilation.

JÍMÚTAVÁHANA (*to himself*).

Good luck ! I have attained my desire.

GARUDA (*seizing the hero*).

Although this protector of the Snakes seems to me

---

* This wish, to a Buddhist, would seem the *ne plus ultra* of self-sacrifice, since to escape from the necessity of future birth, and to obtain nirvána, is the supreme end of their system.

more like a human being, still verily he shall satiate to-day my hunger for snake-flesh. So I will take him and ascend the Malayan mountain, there to eat him at my pleasure.

[*Exeunt omnes.*

END OF FOURTH ACT OF THE NÁGÁNANDA.

ACT V.

Then enters a DOORKEEPER.

DOORKEEPER.

Through affection, one fears danger to a beloved object, even if he be only gone into the garden of his own house; how much more, when placed in the midst of an awful forest, whose mighty dangers are well known. The mighty king Viśvávasu sits in sorrow, saying to himself, "Jímútaváhana, who is gone to see the ocean's shore, stops a long time;" and he has given me these orders—"Since, O Sunanda! I have heard that my son-in-law, Jímútaváhana, has gone to the district rendered terrible by the proximity of Garuda, I am fearful for him. Go, then, and ascertain quickly whether he has returned to his own house or not." So I am now going thither. (*Walking about, and looking before him.*) Here is the royal sage, Jímútakétu, Jímútaváhana's father, standing in the compound of his hut, respectfully attended by his wife and the king's daughter. See!

Jímútaketu has a splendour like the ocean, wearing as he does two linen garments, with ripples tremulous as waves and white as the ocean's foam, and adorned by his queen, as the ocean is by the Ganges, each alike possessed of great holiness, and abundant in maternal streams; and at their side shines Malayavatí, like the ocean's shore. I will go up to them.

Then enters King JÍMÚTAKETU, *with his wife and daughter-in-law.*

KING.

I have enjoyed all the pleasures of youth, and held sway in a kingdom full of glory; I have steadily exercised devotion; my son is of great renown, and my daughter-in-law here is of fitting parentage; now that all my desires are fulfilled, should I not contemplate death?

DOORKEEPER (*coming up suddenly*).

—Of Jímútaváhana—

KING (*stopping his ears*).

Cease! An ill-omen!*

QUEEN.

May this ill-omen be averted!

MALAYAVATÍ.

This bad omen causes my heart to palpitate.

---

* The utterance by the doorkeeper of the genitive case of Jímútaváhana, immediately succeeding, as it does, the word "death," uttered by the king, forms an inauspicious omen.

KING

(starting as though he felt a throbbing of the left eye).
Good sir, what of Jímútaváhana ?

DOORKEEPER.

I am sent to you by king Visvávasu to learn tidings
of Jímútaváhana.

KING.

Is not my child there with him ?

QUEEN *(sorrowfully).*

O king ! if he is not there, where can my boy be
gone ?

KING.

Assuredly he will be gone somewhere for our benefit.

MALAYAVATÍ *(with grief, to herself).*

I dread something very different, from the non-appear-
ance of my husband.

DOORKEEPER.

Give your orders. What message am I to take my
lord ?

KING

(starting as though he felt a throbbing of the left eye).

I am perfectly bewildered in my mind with the
thought that Jímútaváhana delays so long. Why do
you keep throbbing, O left eye, again and again, indicat-
ing some evil as about to happen ? Base that you are,
yonder sun shall stop your throbbings. *(Looking up.)*

Yonder bright thousand-rayed one, sole eye of the three worlds, shall soon bring to light the happiness of Jímú-taváhana. (*Looking astonished.*) What is this that has suddenly fallen in front of me from the sky? as it were a star, loosened by a portentous wind, shooting forth red streaks, bright as rays, and giving excessive pain to the eye of the beholder. How is this? It has fallen at my very feet. (*All look at it.*) Alas! it is a crest-jewel, with moist flesh adhering to it! Whose can it be!

QUEEN (*in a tone of distress*).

O king! it is the crest-jewel of my poor boy.

MALAYAVATÍ.

O mother! say not so.

DOORKEEPER.

O king! do not distress yourself through ignorance of facts. In this place many crest-jewels of the chiefs of the Nágas, who are devoured by Garuda, fall torn off by his beak and claws.

KING.

O queen! there is some reason in what he says. I hope that it may prove so!

QUEEN.

O Sunanda! assuredly by this time my son will have arrived at his father-in-law's house from that shore. Go, then, and ascertain for us quickly.

DOORKEEPER.

As the queen orders.

[*Exit.*

KING.

O queen! would that it might prove to be the crest of a Nága.

Then enters S'ANKHACHÚDA, *clad in red garments.*

S'ANKHACHÚDA (*shedding tears*).

After hastily paying my respects at the shrine of Gokarna, on the ocean's shore, I am again come to this slaughter-house of the Nágas. But Garuda has taken that Vidyádhara, after tearing open his breast with his beak and claws, and is flown up towards heaven. (*Sobbing.*) Alas! Thou excessively magnanimous and affectionate one! Alas! My only true friend, though indeed thou hadst no cause to be so! Alas! Thou that sufferest for another's sake, whither art thou gone? Give me an answer. Alas! Base S'ankhachúda, thou art utterly undone, since thou hast not obtained the merit of saving the Nágas, even for one day, nor even the praiseworthiness arising from obedience to thy lord's commands. Thou art to be pitied, since thou hast been saved at the expense of another, who gave up his life for thine. Woe! Woe! How thou hast been deceived! How thou hast been deceived! This being the state of things, I will not live to be made a laughing-stock, but will at once endeavour to follow him. (*Walking about, and looking intently on the ground.*) I proceed, full of desire to see Garuda, tracking carefully this line of blood, which, through its purple hue, is hard to be traced on this rock, which is variegated with minerals, and rendered obscure by the thick trees. At first the track is broad, as if from the sudden gush, and then the drops become clotted, and at wider intervals; next, a few drops are seen, scattered among the stones in a broken line, and then they are full of insects on the level ground.

QUEEN (*with alarm*).

O king! this man, coming hither hastily, with his face flushed, appears troubled, and fills my heart with alarm. Let us ascertain who he is.

KING.

As the queen says. (*Listening; with joy, and smiling.*) O queen! cease from sorrow. Assuredly this crest-jewel must be his, let fall on this spot by some bird, who snatched it from his head, thinking from its colour that it was a piece of flesh.

QUEEN (*joyfully, embracing* MALAYAVATÍ).

O thou saved from widowhood, be calm. Such a form as this was not made to suffer the pains of widowhood.

MALAYAVATÍ (*with joy*).

O mother! it must be then through the efficacy of thy blessing.

[*Falls at her feet.*

KING (*to* S'ANKHACHÚDA).

My child, what is the matter?

S'ANKHACHÚDA.

My throat being obstructed with tears through the excess of my grief, I am totally unable to tell you.

KING.

My son, tell me thy sorrow, that it may become more endurable from participation. At present it is intolerable, while shut up in thine own heart.

SANKHACHÚDA.

Hear it, then. I am a Nága, Sankhachúda by name. I was sent by Vásuki, as a meal for Garuda. But why waste time in words? Even as we talk, perhaps these tracks of drops of blood mingled with dust are disappearing. I will therefore tell it in a breath. By a certain Vidyádhara, whose mind was full of compassion, my life has been preserved. He has given himself up to Garuda.

KING.

Who else would thus undergo calamity for another? My child, you might as well have said at once, " By Jímútaváhana!" Alas! I am undone, ill-fated man that I am.

QUEEN.

Alas! my child, how could you do this?

MALAYAVATÍ.

How true has my foreboding proved!

[*They all faint.*

SANKHACHÚDA (*with tears*).

Surely these must be the parents of that magnanimous one, otherwise they would not be brought into this condition by my evil tidings. But what else should issue from the mouth of a venomous serpent, except poison?

Assuredly, S'ankhachúda has worthily repaid his bene-
factor! In what way, now, shall I put an end to myself?
But I must first revive these two. Revive, my father!
Cheer up, O mother!

> [*They both revive.*

QUEEN.

Stand up, my child. Do not weep. Shall we live
without Jimútaváhana? Cheer up, then.

MALAYAVATÍ (*recovering*).

O husband! where shall I see you again?

KING.

Alas! O my child, who knew so well how to perform
the duty of honouring thy father's feet, even in another
world the practice of good behaviour is not forgotten by
thee, since thou hast dropped thy crest-jewel at my feet.
(*Takes up the crest-jewel.*) Alas! my child, is it only in
this way that I can now behold thee? (*Puts it to his
breast.*) Alas! Alas! O thou, whose head was continually bowed at my feet in constant devotion, thy
crest-jewel, polished by their contact as by a touchstone,
was never guilty of injuring any one; why, then, does it
now rudely pierce my breast?

QUEEN.

Alas! my son Jímútaváhana, whose only pleasure
was in obedience to thy father, how could'st thou leave
him, and go to enjoy the delights of heaven?

KING (*with tears*).

O queen! can we live without Jímútaváhana, that
you talk thus?

MALAYAVATÍ
(falling at his feet, and clasping her hands).

Give me the crest-jewel, as a memorial of my husband, that, wearing it in my bosom, I may mount the funeral pile, and quench my burning sorrows in the fire.

KING.

O devoted one! why do you thus trouble me? Is not this the fixed determination of us all?

QUEEN.

O King, why do we then delay?

KING.

There is no reason. But one, who has always maintained a sacred fire, obtains purification from no other. Therefore, we will fetch fire from the sacred fire-cell, and burn ourselves.*

S'ANKHACHÚDA *(to himself).*

Alas! for the sake of me, a single individual, this whole family of Vidyádharas is utterly destroyed. I will see what can be done. *(Aloud.)* O father, not without due deliberation should such a rash purpose be carried out. The sportings of destiny demand thought. Perhaps, when he finds that he is not a Nága, the enemy of the Nágas will let him go again. Let us then follow Garuda in this direction.

* Compare Colebrooke's Essays, I., page 157. At the obsequies of a priest, who maintained a consecrated fire, his funeral pile must be lighted from that fire.

F

QUEEN.

It will assuredly be by the special favour of the gods if we look on the face of our son, yet living.

MALAYAVATÍ (to herself).

Most assuredly I, ill-fated that I am, can hardly look for such a blessing.

KING.

O child, may this speech * of thine prove true! Still it is fitting that we should take the fires with us, as we follow. Do you, then, follow the track; and we will come as soon as we have brought the fire from the fire-cell.

[*Exit, with wife and daughter-in-law.*

S'ANKHACHÚDA.

I will now follow Garuda. (*Looking in front.*) Yonder, afar off, I see the enemy of the Nágas, on a pinnacle of Malaya, making new gulleys in the mountain-side, as he rubs his gory beak. The woods around are all uprooted and burnt by the streaks of flaming fire from his eyes, and the ground is hollowed round him by his dreadful adamantine claws.

Then enters GARUDA, seated on a rock, with the hero lying in front of him.

GARUDA.

Never since my birth has so wonderful a thing been seen by me in my feasts on the lords of the Nágas! Not

* This of course is said in answer to S'ankhachúda's suggestion above.

only is this hero unterrified, but he even appears almost delighted. There is no lassitude seen in him, though most of his blood is drunk up. His face, through its heroic endurance, even when he is suffering the pangs from the tearing of his flesh, seems serene as in ecstacy. Every limb, which is not actually destroyed, bristles with rapture. His glance falls on me, whilst doing him an injury, as though I were doing him a favour. Hence, by his heroism, my curiosity is excited. I will not eat him. I will ask who he is.

JÍMÚTAVÁHANA.

There is yet flesh in my body, whose blood pours forth from every vein; and you, O magnanimous one, do not seem satiated. Why, then, O Garuda, do you stop eating?

GARUDA (to himself).

Wonder of wonders! How! Even in this state does he still speak thus stoutly! (Aloud.) This heroism of thine seems to call back the heart's blood that has been poured out by my beak. I wish, then, to hear who thou art.

JÍMÚTAVÁHANA.

It is not fit that you should hear, while tormented by hunger. Satiate yourself, then, with my flesh and blood.

S'ANKHACHÚDA (coming up in haste).

O Garuda, not indeed, not indeed should this cruelty be done. This is no Nága. Let him go. Eat me. I am sent by Vásuki for thy food.

[Presents his breast.

JÍMÚTAVÁHANA (*on seeing* SANKHACHÚDA).

Alas! my desire has become fruitless through the arrival of Sankhachúda.

GARUDA (*looking at them both*).

Both of you wear the distinctive badge of victims. Which is really the Nága I know not.

SANKHACHÚDA.

The error is a likely one, forsooth. Not to mention the mark of the Swastika * on the breast, are there not the scales on my body? Do you not count my two tongues as I speak? Nor see these three hoods of mine, the compressed wind hissing through them in my insupportable anguish? While the brightness of my gems is distorted by the thick smoke from the fire of my direful poison.

GARUDA (*looking at both, and noticing the hood of* SANKHACHÚDA).

Who, then, is this that I have destroyed?

SANKHACHÚDA.

It is Jímútaváhana, the ornament of the race of Vidyádharas. How was this done by thee, O merciless one?

GARUDA (*to himself*).

Ah! How, indeed, was it done? This, then, is that

---

* "Swastika" is a mystical figure in the form of a cross. This passage might serve as a "*locus classicus*" for the Hindu conception of a Nága. Mr Fergusson gives pictures, taken from sculptures, of Nágas with three, five, or seven hoods.

Jímútaváhana, prince of the Vidyádharas, whose fame I have repeatedly heard sung by the hosts of bards who traverse Lokáloka,* sung on the slopes of Meru, in the caves of Mandara, on the table-land of Himavat, on mount Mahendra, on the peaks of Kailása, even on these heights of Malaya, and in the various caverns of the mountains that bound the world. Of a truth, I am plunged in a vast quagmire of iniquity!

JÍMÚTAVÁHANA.

O lord of snakes, why art thou thus troubled?

SANKHACHÚDA.

Is it not a time for excessive trouble? If my body were preserved from Garuda by the sacrifice of thine, verily it were right that thou shouldst hurl me to a depth lower than the deepest hell.

GARUDA.

Alas! alas! His own body has been of his own accord presented for my food by this noble-minded one, through pity, to save the life of a Nága, who had fallen within the reach of my voracity. What a terrible sin then have I committed! In a word, this is a "Bodhi-sattwa,"† whom I have slain. I see no way of expiating my sin, except by entering the fire. Where then shall

* "Lokáloka," a mountainous chain surrounding the outermost of the seven seas, and which bounds the world, with the Hindus.

† "Bodhi-sattwa" is a technical term in Buddhist theology, denoting a potential Buddha, or one who has only one more birth remaining before he becomes a perfect Buddha, and meanwhile waits in heaven until his period comes round.

I find fire? (*Looking round.*) Ah! Here come some with fire. I will wait till they arrive.

S'ANKHACHÚDA.

O prince, your parents are come.

JÍMÚTAVÁHANA (*with agitation*).

O Śankhachúda, do you sit down, and conceal my body with my upper garment. Otherwise, perhaps, my mother might die, if she suddenly saw me in this state.

> [S'ANKHACHÚDA *takes up the garment fallen at his side, and does so.*

Then enters KING JÍMÚTAKETU, *with his wife and daughter-in-law.*

KING (*sorrowfully*).

Alas! son Jímútaváhana, whence came this exalted degree of compassion—"Another is as one's-self?" How was it that the thought did not occur to you—"Are many to be saved, or one?" For, by giving up your life to save a Nága from Garuda, yourself, your parents, your wife, yea the whole family is destroyed.

QUEEN (*addressing* MALAYAVATÍ).

O daughter, desist. You will extinguish the fire with your incessant tears.

> [*All walk round.*

KING.

Alas! my son Jímútaváhana!

GARUDA (*on hearing this*).

He says—"Alas! my son Jímútaváhana!" This then is doubtless his father. How can I burn myself in this fire? I am ashamed to appear before them after slaying their son. Yet why should I be troubled about a fire? Am not I on the ocean's brink? I will cast myself into the submarine fire,* terrible as the destined consumer of the world at the end of a "kalpa," having kindled it by the wind of my own wings, fiercer than any supernatural blast, which will make the flames flicker like the tips of the tongue of Death, when enjoying the relish of licking up the three worlds, and which span the sea, and reach even to threaten the sun's domain.

[*He wishes to rise.*

JÍMÚTAVÁHANA.

O king of birds, away with this resolve! This would be no expiation for your sin.

GARUDA (*falling on his knees, and putting his hands together*).

O magnanimous one, tell me then what expiation is there?

---

* "Vádava," or submarine fire. "In Hindu mythology this is represented as a being consisting of flame, but with the head of a mare, who sprang from the thigh of Úrva, and was received by the ocean."—*Wilson's Dictionary.* He is also called Aurva Bhárgava. He will destroy the world at the end of the "kalpa" or aeon. The Brahmanical "kalpa" consists of four thousand, three hundred, and twenty millions of solar years.

JÍMÚTAVÁHANA.

Wait a moment. My parents are come. I will first pay my respects to them.

GARUDA.

Do so.

KING (*with joy, having seen him*).

O queen, fortune favours you! Here is our son Jímútaváhana, not only alive, but respectfully waited on by Garuda, with his hands folded like a disciple.

QUEEN.

O mighty king, my desires are all accomplished. I shall see his face, and surely his body must be uninjured.

MALAYAVATÍ.

Even though I see my husband, I cannot believe it. It is too dear to be true!

KING (*going up*).

Come, my child, embrace me.
          [JÍMÚTAVÁHANA *wishing to rise, the garment*
          falls off, and he faints.

S'ANKHACHÚDA.

O prince, revive, revive!

KING.

Alas! my child, having seen me, are you gone without an embrace?

QUEEN.

Alas! my child, do you not greet me with a single word?

MALAYAVATÍ.

Alas! my husband, are not even your parents worthy of a glance?

[*They all faint.*

SANKHACHÚDA (*to himself*).

O villain Sankhachúda, why did you not perish, whilst yet unborn? Seeing that moment by moment you endure pangs worse than death itself!

GARUDA.

All this is caused by my inconsiderate action. Base wretch that I am! But I will do what I can. (*Fanning with his wings.*) O noble one, revive, revive!

JÍMÚTAVÁHANA (*recovering*).

O Sankhachúda, revive my parents.

SANKHACHÚDA.

O father, recover! O mother, revive!

[*Both come to their senses.*

QUEEN.

O son, does that villain Death carry you off in our very sight?

KING.

O queen, speak not so inauspiciously. The long-lived one * yet breathes. See to his wife.

* Áyushmán, long-lived one, is here used as an address of good omen, and implies an understood prayer. It is a favourite Buddhist expression.

QUEEN

(*weeping, having covered her face with her dress*).

The omen be averted! I will not weep. O Malayavatí, revive. Rise, my child, rise. At this time, if ever, look on the face of thy husband.

MALAYAVATÍ (*coming to herself*).

Alas! my husband!

QUEEN (*stopping the mouth of* MALAYAVATÍ).

O child, act not thus. May this omen be averted.

KING (*to himself, with tears*).

Why do I not burst into a hundred pieces through sorrow, as I behold my son giving up his life, which, the rest of his body being destroyed, has retreated to his throat as to its last remaining stronghold?

MALAYAVATÍ.

Alas! my husband! I must indeed be very wicked, since, even when I see my husband in such a state, I yet live on!

QUEEN (*stroking the limbs of the hero, and addressing* GARUDA).

O thou who fearest naught, how could this body of my son, in the fresh bloom of youth, be brought by thee to such a state as this?

JÍMÚTAVÁHANA.

O mother, not so indeed. What harm has been done by him? Was it not in reality just the same before?

See. What beauty can there be in a body, loathsome to the sight, and consisting of blood, marrow, flesh, bones, and fat, covered in by skin ?

GARUDA.

O noble-minded one, I stand in pain, regarding myself as already consumed by the fiery flames of hell. Point out, then, I pray, how I can be cleansed from my guilt.

JÍMÚTAVÁHANA.

If my father gives me leave, I will point out the expiation for this fault.

KING.

Do so, my child.

JÍMÚTAVÁHANA.

Listen then, Garuda.

GARUDA (*putting his hands together*).

Give your instructions.

JÍMÚTAVÁHANA.

Cease for ever from destroying life; repent of thy former deeds; labour to gather together an unbroken chain of good actions, by inspiring confidence in all living beings; so that this sin, which has its origin in the destruction of living beings, may not ripen to bear fruit, but may be all absorbed in thy merits, as a morsel of salt thrown into the depths of yonder ocean.

GARUDA.

Whatever you order. I, who was lying in a sleep of

ignorance, now, awakened by you, have from this day ceased from destroying living beings. Now let the race of Nágas wander happily in the mighty ocean—at times stretching from shore to shore like bridges—at times taken for whirlpools, through the coiling of their bodies—and at times resembling continents, from the multitude of their hoods, large as alluvial islands. Again, let the damsels of the Nágas in yon grove of sandal trees celebrate joyfully this glory of thine, thinking lightly of the fatigue, though their bodies faint with the exertion, and though their cheeks, browned by the touch of the rays of the early sun, seem as if bedaubed with red lead, while their hair let fall to their feet resembles the darkness of clouds.

Jímútaváhana.

Well said, O magnanimous one! We are delighted. By all means keep firm to your purpose. (*Addressing* Sankhachúda.) O Sankhachúda, do you now go home.

[Sankhachúda, *sighing, stands with downcast looks.*

Jímútaváhana (*sighing as he looks at his mother*).

For assuredly thy mother will be sitting full of grief for thy pain, as she looks up, expecting to see thee drop, mangled by Garuda's beak.

Queen (*with tears*).

Blessed indeed is that mother, who will behold the face of her son, with his body uninjured, though he was actually in the very jaws of Garuda.

S'ANKHACHÚDA.

O mother, it is indeed as you say. Would that the Prince might be saved !

JÍMÚTAVÁHANA (*speaking as though in agony*).

Ah ! oh ! These joint-racking pangs were not felt by me before, through the excess of pleasure, which I felt in doing good to another, but now they begin to hem me round.

[*He sinks in a dying state.*

KING (*with agitation*).

Alas ! my son, why this posture ?

QUEEN.

Alas ! alas ! Why does he talk thus ? (*Beating her breast.*) Help ! help ! My child is dying !

MALAYAVATÍ.

Ah ! my husband, you appear in a hurry to leave us. '

JÍMÚTAVÁHANA (*trying to place his hands together*).
O S'ankhachúda ! place my hands together.

S'ANKHACHÚDA (*doing so*).
Alas ! the world is robbed of its master.

JÍMÚTAVÁHANA (*half opening his eyes, and looking at his father*).

O father, O mother ! This is my last salutation. These limbs retain no consciousness—my ear hears no sound, however distinct the articulation—alas ! my eye is fast closing—my father, these vital airs are quickly leaving me in my powerlessness—but, "Through the merit that I gain to-day by protecting a Nága at the sacrifice of myself, may I still obtain in succeeding existences a body to be sacrificed for others."*

[*He falls.*

QUEEN.

Alas, my son! Alas, my child! Alas, darling of thy parents! Where art thou? Tell me!

KING.

Alas, child Jímútaváhana! Alas, the darling of thy companions! Alas, thou possessed of all virtues, where art thou? Tell me! (*Throwing up his hands.*) Alas! alas! woe! Firmness has now no home. To whom can modesty go for protection? Who in the whole world now possesses patience? Liberality has ceased, and truth has verily perished! Whither now can pity go, itself worthy of pity? The whole world has become void by thy departure to another, O my son!

MALAYAVATÍ.

Alas, my husband! How could you leave me and depart? O Malayavatí, how cruel you are! What do you not deserve for living so long after your husband?

S'ANKHACHÚDA.

O Prince, where art thou gone, forsaking these people, dearer to thee than life itself? Assuredly now S'ankachúda will follow thee.

* He repeats this sentence from the end of the fourth act, where Garuda first seizes him.

GARUDA.

Alas! This noble-minded one is dead. What shall I now do?

QUEEN (*looking up with tears*).

Oh revered guardians of the world, bring my son to life by sprinkling him in some way with ambrosia.

GARUDA (*joyfully to himself*).

Ah! The mention of ambrosia reminds me opportunely. I think I may yet wipe out my disgrace. I will pray to Indra, and persuade him by a shower of ambrosia to restore to life not only Jímútaváhana, but all those lords of Nágas that have heretofore been eaten by me, and who are now merely skeletons. If he will not grant it, then,—having drunk up the ocean with my wings, and borne along by mighty winds of ever-increasing violence, while the twelve suns fall fainting, bewildered by the flaming fierceness of my eyes.—I will break to pieces with my beak the thunderbolt of Indra, the club of Kuvera, and the staff of Yama, the lord of the dead, and, having conquered the Gods in battle, will at once by my own might let fall an ambrosial shower. Here, then, I go.

[*Exit, after walking round haughtily.*

KING.

O child, S'ankhachúḍa, why do you still delay? Collect wood, and build a funeral pile for my son, that we too may go with him.

QUEEN.

O son, S'ankhachúda, quickly get it ready. Thy brother remains in pain, without our company.

S'ANKHACHÚDA (*tearfully*).

Whatever my parents order. Am not I willing to lead the way? (*Rises and builds a funeral pile.*) O father, O mother, here is the funeral pile prepared.

KING.

O Queen, why do you still weep? Rise, we will mount the pile.

[*All stand up.*

ι. MALAYAVATÍ (*looking up with her hands together*).

O revered Gaurí, it was promised by thee—"An emperor of the Vidyádharas shall be thy husband." How, then, in my case, wretched one that I am, have thy words proved untrue ?

(*Then enters* GAURÍ, *as in haste.*)

GAURÍ.

O mighty King Jímútaketu, assuredly this rash act must not be done.

KING.

Oh! How can the sight of Gaurí be in vain ?

GAURÍ (*addressing* MALAYAVATÍ).

Child, how could I prove untrue ? (*Going up to the hero, and sprinkling him with water from a water-pot.*) I am well pleased with thee, who even at the cost of thy

own life would'st benefit the world.   Live, Jimútaváhana !

> [*The hero stands up.*

KING (*joyfully*).

O Queen ! joy ! joy !   Our son is restored to life!

QUEEN.

By the blessing of Gaurí.

JÍMÚTAVÁHANA
(*having seen* GAURÍ, *putting his hands together*).

Ah ! how should the sight of Gaurí be in vain ?   O
thou who grantest all desires, and removest all pain from
thy prostrate worshippers, O protectress, I bow at thy
feet,—O Gaurí, ever celebrated in song by the Vidyádharas !

> [*He falls at the feet of* GAURÍ.

All look upwards.

KING.

Ah ! what means this shower, when no clouds are
seen ?   O revered one, what is this ?

GAURÍ.

O King Jímútaketu, this shower of ambrosia is caused
to fall by the repentant lord of birds, to restore to life
Jímútaváhana, and these lords of the Nágas, now only
skeletons.   (*Pointing with a finger.*)   Do you not see
these lords of Nágas ?   Now they reach S'ankhachúda,
their heads bright with the rays of their unveiled crest-
jewels—now they lick up the very ground in their haste

to devour the ambrosia with their two-forked tongues—
and now, hurrying along, they plunge into the ocean by
tortuous paths, like the waters of the rivers of the Malaya
hills.   (*Addressing the hero.*)   O child Jimútaváhana,
thou art worthy of something more than the mere gift
of life, therefore this is my further blessing to thee—I
on this very spot will make thee in a moment an universal emperor of the Vidyádharas, having sprinkled
thee with purifying waters produced ready at hand from
my Mánasa lake, only sullied by the dust of the golden
lotuses, shaken by the pinions of the wild geese,—and
placed in jewelled jars created by my will.   Let the
jewel of the golden wheel come first, then the elephant
with the four white tusks, and the dark coloured horse,
and next Malayavatí.*   O emperor, behold these are the
the jewels which I give thee.   Yet further,—behold
these nobles of the Vidyádharas, bearing in their hands
chowries of the yak's tail, white as the autumnal moon,
making, as they walk, and bow, and bend their bodies
low in devotion, very rainbows with the rays of their
gems,—and among them the villain Matanga and his
fellows.   Tell me, now, what yet further boon I can
grant thee?

JIMÚTAVÁHANA.

What boon can there be beyond this?   S'ankhachúda
is delivered from him who was the dread of all the
snakes; Garuda has been brought to a better mind;
all the lords of the Nágas, whom he had ever eaten,

---

* The wheel, the elephant, the horse, and the queen, are four of
the seven jewels (ratnáni) which distinguish the universal emperor
(Chakravartin) among the Buddhists. See Lalita-Vistara, III.

he has now restored to life; my parents are yet alive, through the recovery of my life; imperial dignity has been obtained; and thou, O goddess, hast been seen visibly present. What further boon can I ask of thee? Yet, grant that these words of Bharata may come true:—May the clouds in due season let loose their showers, exhilarating the pea-fowl in their wild dance. May they clothe the earth with green harvests in a continual succession! And may all my subjects, accumulating good works, and freed from all calamities, rejoice with minds untainted by envy, tasting unbroken pleasure in the society of relations and friends!

[*Exeunt omnes.*

END OF FIFTH AND LAST ACT.

ADDITIONAL NOTES.

Page 1, line 9.

The words which I render "Buddha, the conqueror," are *Buddho Jinah*.

"Le nom de *Djina* est un des synonymes de celui de *Buddha*, ou plutôt c'est un des nombreuses épithètes que l'on donne à un Buddha. Il signifie *vainqueur* dans un sens moral et religieux. On sait qu'il est commun aux Buddhistes et aux Djainas."—BURNOUF

Page 20, line 18.

I have translated *chandana-latá* as "sandal-creeper," as the St Petersburg Dictionary only explains *latá* by "Schlinggewachs," "Ranke;" but the sandal-tree is not properly a creeper. *Santalum album* is described by Roxburgh as having a stem only a few feet high; it then divides into numerous branches, which spread and rise in every direction, forming nearly a spherical head. *Latá*, therefore, seems to be used here to express the spreading branches of any tree which can be formed into a bower.

The *Santalum album* is found in the mountainous parts of Malabar. Dr Buchanan (*Journey* II. 536) says that it does not grow on the coast, but is found on the eastern side of the western Ghâts. The *Santalum* (or *sirium*) *myrtifolium* appears to be a different tree. Roxburgh describes it as a "native of the Circar mountains, where it is but of a small size, and the wood of little or no value."

PRINTED BY BALLANTYNE AND COMPANY
EDINBURGH AND LONDON

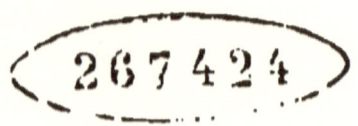